'*Cherry Beach* is a tender and bruising coming-of-age novel. Laura McPhee-Browne economical, finely at n of youth, unfamil
JE

'Laura McPhee-Br *Cherry Beach* is an acute and gripping novel about being made and unmade by first love. In prose reminiscent of Elizabeth Jolley's, McPhee-Browne portrays the helpless entanglement of two friends in their impossible quest for self-determination. *Cherry Beach* is a breathtaking debut by a gifted new voice in Australian fiction.'
ELLENA SAVAGE

'This beautiful novel is tender: tender like a loving touch, and tender like a bruise. *Cherry Beach* will seduce you with its lush and gorgeous detail and its unguarded openness, and then it will rip your heart out. In its rawness and its yearning, *Cherry Beach* exquisitely captures the intensity of youth, love, desire and loss.'
EMILY BITTO

'Like sparkling wine on a sunny afternoon, *Cherry Beach* goes down easily—and leaves a killer hangover. A vibrant, tender debut from a bright new voice in Australian fiction. I loved every minute of it.'
LAURA ELIZABETH WOOLLETT

'A promising debut…[*Cherry Beach* explores] mental health, female friendship and desire, delicately portraying the deep ache of losing the person you're closest to.'
BOOKS+PUBLISHING

CHERRY BEACH

Laura McPhee-Browne is a writer and social worker living in Melbourne, on Wurundjeri land. Her short stories have been published widely in Australia. Laura also volunteers as a fiction editor for the literary magazine *Verity La*. *Cherry Beach* is her first novel.

lauramcpheebrowne.com

CHERRY BEACH

LAURA McPHEE-BROWNE

TEXT PUBLISHING MELBOURNE AUSTRALIA

textpublishing.com.au

The Text Publishing Company
Swann House, 22 William Street, Melbourne Victoria 3000, Australia

Copyright © Laura McPhee-Browne, 2020

The moral right of Laura McPhee-Browne to be identified as the author of this work has been asserted.

All rights reserved. Without limiting the rights under copyright above, no part of this publication shall be reproduced, stored in or introduced into a retrieval system, or transmitted in any form or by any means (electronic, mechanical, photocopying, recording or otherwise), without the prior permission of both the copyright owner and the publisher of this book.

Published by The Text Publishing Company, 2020

Book design by Imogen Stubbs
Cover painting by Emma Currie
Typeset by J&M Typesetting

Printed and bound in Australia by Griffin Press, part of Ovato, an accredited ISO/NZS 14001:2004 Environmental Management System printer

ISBN: 9781922268501 (paperback)
ISBN: 9781925923117 (ebook)

A catalogue record for this book is available from the National Library of Australia

 This book is printed on paper certified against the Forest Stewardship Council® Standards. Griffin Press holds FSC chain-of-custody certification SGS-COC-005088. FSC promotes environmentally responsible, socially beneficial and economically viable management of the world's forests.

*For my grandparents, Helen and Max,
and for my oldest friend, Isabel*

Not Much of Anything but Open Water   *1*

Sâkahikan   *5*

Lac   *10*

Channel   *19*

Oasis   *23*

Wash   *31*

Rip   *41*   Tributary   *107*

Dam   *47*   Creek   *115*

Mouth   *55*   Kettle   *122*

Ria   *66*   Seep   *127*

Cove   *73*   Sound   *133*

Well   *81*   Brackish   *140*

Mere   *93*   Pool   *156*

Wetland   *103*   Meander   *163*

Lake   *173*

Sea   *177*

Glacier   *186*

Yarro-Yarro   *191*

A Billabong Is a Dead River   *209*

And indeed I remember believing
As a child, I could walk on water—
The next wave, the next wave—
It was only a matter of balance.

Gwen Harwood, 'At Mornington'

> Our love and our love alone
> Keeps dowsing for water.
> Sinking the well of each other, digging together.
> Each one the other's phantom limb in the sea.
>
> *Marin Sorescu, 'Fountains in the Sea'*
> *(translated by Seamus Heaney)*

Not Much of Anything but Open Water

It is very cold, and the wind flays my cheeks as I walk down Cherry Street. I don't know if I can like it down here. It's industrial and lonely until you get to the beach car park and see the water, and there are hardly ever any other people to make you feel like you are still a part of something. Someone told me that the police used to take people down here after they picked them up so they could punish them with abandon, in peace. I can imagine that, that power in the dark, with only the noise of the water to drown the body blows.

When I walked down to Cherry Beach in spring, I passed the Mini Blossom Park and saw the cherry blossoms. They were so happy—puffs of breath and grandmother hair. It's early winter now, and I can see as I near the little park that the trees are naked and cold. The grandmother hair is in my head these days. It feels puffy and woolly and stuck, and I didn't get to do what I planned to do today because I couldn't push through the thick of it.

The new tattoo on my back hurts. I wonder if it needs some

cream and a bandage. I don't remember getting it, but that's not surprising. There are blanks, these days, between the light. I almost like the way I don't seem to have to deal with the whole of anything anymore. I could see the shape of the wound in the mirror when I turned away, looking over my shoulder. My back is clean and bony. It will always be like this.

I can hear the lapping of the water, wet and gentle against the sand, and can smell rocks and stones. Beyond that is the almost-moan you can hear if you listen closely to an ocean at night, from all the things that are happening beneath its surface. *Move closer*, says the voice that is always with me now: *Move closer. You deserve it. Move closer.*

I want to spread out across the water and let my body become wavy and romantic. My hair will tendril and float like a long sea plant. It is alive and so is the water, but this city doesn't feel alive like that anymore. I know the salt will refresh me; I have been needing refreshment for so long. Water washes away what people are thinking and all the wool and pulse in my head, even when I am just in the shower or beneath rain clouds without an umbrella. I'll swim for a long time to really clean it all away. I don't think it will be as cold in the sea as it is out here in the air.

I have reached the car park. There is a high street lamp above me, pouring white light across the gravel. There are no cars, but plenty of tyre tracks and littered chip packets. I can see a sock and a pair of sandals someone has left to die alone. The sock is frozen. I pick it up and crunch it a little to feel something between my fingers—I like the delicate slices of ice that coat it. Someone wore this on their foot, once, not that long ago. I am wearing two pairs of socks: one blue burly pair and one white cotton pair with dirty soles. My feet are still cold.

The sand is cool and wet when I pick some up to let it go. I imagine I am the sand and someone is picking me up and letting me go, scattering every grain of me below them. I pull off my coat and my boots. I walk towards the ocean; I dive.

SÂKAHIKAN
cree for lake

We arrived on a Tuesday, I can remember that. I can remember Hetty's hand in mine as we moved slowly down the steps of the escalator, as if standing completely still would have been harder than moving. It was cold even in the airport: the first time I realised how cold can seep through. I remember Hetty's hand was cold too, and that she felt tired next to me. We'd been in the sky breathing fake air for longer than a normal day and night. Hetty's long body couldn't fall asleep in an aeroplane chair, and the only movie we could both agree to watch together—with our separate plastic headphones—was a French film with lots of boring silent bits and close-ups of skinny faces.

It was a relief to stretch and stand, free and wide on the lino in the airport, and to feel like we were nearly where we had wanted to be for so long. I remember that the chewing gum in my mouth had lost all of its flavour, that my jaw hurt from moving up and down, but that I kept it in the corner of my mouth as the only familiar thing. I was standing on the edge of something, next to Hetty but a little bit alone, and it could have been a cliff or a diving board. The only difference was that I didn't feel scared.

That crackling, swirling feeling of being somewhere completely new was in me as we waited for our bags. We'd tied red ribbons to our luggage so that we would recognise it among the grey and khaki and black, and it came quickly. We took everything as an omen back then, Hetty and I, and told each other as we walked to the taxi bay that it was a sign—our bags had arrived first because we were meant to be there. Hetty had her long dark hair pulled back and her face was clean and bright, even though she was wilting. I hadn't looked in the mirror since we'd left Melbourne—I shrugged off grooming as if it was a waste of effort, and didn't try to make myself look better. My thick eyebrows, the cross-over of my front teeth, the woolly hair that sat unbrushed against my shoulders: these were my messages to the world that I didn't care, that I wasn't the kind of person who worried about what others thought of them. I can see now that this was just a different type of vanity.

'It doesn't feel real,' Hetty said. We were waiting for a taxi, breath coming out of our mouths in huffs. 'It's like we're not actually here yet.'

I knew what she meant. Dark took away the edge of a place, and it was after midnight. The airport was busy but no one was looking at us, and I couldn't hear anyone talking above a low murmur. I had been looking forward to hearing the Canadian accent all around me, but I'd heard nothing. There wasn't anything yet to compare ourselves to, to stand separate from.

'Maybe we're not. No one actually said, Welcome to Canada.'

I crossed my eyes and poked out my tongue, and Hetty laughed and shivered in her coat, jumping up and down a little to warm herself. She was tall, Hetty, as I've said. I was medium, and Hetty was tall in the way that made strangers stop her on the street to see if she was wearing heels. She didn't roll her eyes but preferred to smile and answer that no, no, she'd never played basketball. Didn't like sport at all, really. Wasn't good at it. Hetty was a peacemaker.

Inside the taxi it was close and warm and the driver smiled big at us in his rear-view mirror. We told him where we needed to go—to the house of a couple we'd found on a couch-sharing site offering a room and two beds—and he was so enthusiastic the air was thick with it, along with the candied scent of his air freshener hanging from the mirror in the shape of a red delicious.

'I'm so happy to be able to drive you,' he told us. He was a large man, with rolled-up shirt sleeves, salmon-coloured skin and the air of a new grandfather. He had a whiff of white hair at the top of his head and the skin around it was shining, even in the dark. I thought back to men like this who drove taxis in Melbourne. They never seemed happy to be able to drive me; rather they knew they had to, that they needed to, in order to make it through another work day. That had always felt right to me. I didn't know how to smile enough to make it okay that this man was being so kind.

'I've been driving this cab for twenty-seven years,' he told us, rolling out the words carefully, with a smile at the tip of each of them, as if he loved us, which he couldn't have, and we were important, which we weren't. 'I try to make each passenger feel a little better as they get out than when they got in.'

I decided to smile once more, then look out the window. I wanted to see the city—you could tell something about a place from the drive in to the guts of it from the airport. I didn't want to miss anything. The driver's enthusiasm made him seem malleable. I wondered if he had a wife, or a husband, and if they were bossy. Outside the cab, Toronto was rushing by: a hazy dark-green pan of tree leaves, verandahs and basement windows, almost hidden by the black air. I opened my eyes wider to try to see something.

Hetty was leaning against the window, managing to look as though she was comfortable, despite the turning and bumping and braking. A swell of gladness popped in my heart as I looked at her, reminding myself that she had agreed to come, that she must really love me.

The cab driver was humming, and as we slowed down along a narrow street that had come off a wider one I realised what the song was: 'Killing Me Softly'. I wondered where he had heard it, where it had seeped into the pink of his brain. I wondered whether he knew the lyrics or just the tune. I tried not to hum along with him, above the gasp of the radio. I struggled with displays, of emotion or tenderness. I still do, though now I know how important they can be. Humans like to be shown. It has always been hard for me to take care of a stranger the way Hetty could.

We slowed down to a stop outside a squat apartment building. The driver smiled so wide in the rear-view mirror that I had to smile back, and this time the smiling made me feel excited. I reminded myself that we were here, in another country—really far away. This was what I had been waiting for. We paid the driver, who refused a tip and wished us such luck that it felt like he had handed us a heart. Outside the air was breath and spit.

LAC
french for lake

We were staying with Jo and John. Jo had hair dyed the colour of wet rust, and she maintained heavy eye contact. She looked at us like she wanted us to know she was there, from the moment we walked in with our bags, waving goodbye to our driver from the door as he drove away. She was thin, as though she didn't have time for eating, and wore a cross studded with diamantes around her neck.

'We're so happy to have you stay with us!' Her voice sang out above her partner's as he helped us drag our bags into the living room, directing us to the best place to land them. 'We've been so excited for you to arrive!'

'Thanks so much for having us,' Hetty replied, brightly.

'Oh—your accent!' Jo squealed. I reminded myself to talk as little as possible. Since I'd opened my mouth at the airport to say thank you to Passport Control, I'd been struck by how rural and peculiar the Australian accent sounded against the gentle wash of the Canadian. 'It's so amazing!'

'Ha—thank you. It's ridiculous.' Hetty laughed and stretched her arms out in a way that told me she was relaxed.

'Oh, no—it's not ridiculous at all. No, no, no. I love it.'

Jo eyed us from where she stood next to the couch. John had sat and made himself comfortable. He had small eyes and a thick nose, and creases around his mouth that made it look like he was smiling even when he probably wasn't. Big hands tucked neatly below a big belly, a shy shrub of hair planted at the neck of his shirt. I imagined Jo and John in bed together: stroking each other's bodies, so different from their own. They were alien bodies when you looked at them together. I could already imagine that John kept Jo from spinning out into the night. She was eager to show us something—that she loved her life, that she was a happy person, that we were so welcome. She was humming with the effort of it. I wondered if Hetty could hear it too.

Jo showed us where we would sleep—a large room with curtains already drawn across the window. She stood at the door and asked us questions as we made ourselves comfortable. I wished so much that she would leave, so I could pull back the fabric and look out at Toronto.

'It must be so different here to where you're from, eh?' Jo asked, leaning against the doorframe, eyes sad—as if we had come from a strange and distant planet and could only stay on Earth a short while.

'Different to Australia?' I said.

'Yes, Australia.' She said it in a way I had never heard before—sounding out each syllable like she was learning a new concept, a new word she didn't yet understand.

I looked over at Hetty and saw her smile at Jo and then at the carpet. I was tired, and Jo itched at me with her energy. I wanted to lie with Hetty and stare at the Canadian ceiling, to talk about our hosts and see if she felt as loose as I did.

'Well, I'll leave you to it then, ladies!' Jo said, her teeth smiling bigger than her mouth. She had started to massage her neck with one small, veined hand, and I remembered my own body as I watched her. I saw that Hetty was rubbing at her neck too.

As soon as Jo had shut the door behind her Hetty looked at me with wide eyes and I snuffled into my jumper sleeve.

'Jesus.'

'So intense!' Hetty said.

'Is it just me or did she not know that Australia exists?'

Hetty laughed and fell back onto the mattress. She told me she was too lazy to get undressed and I threw a pillow at her. Lying down on my back I felt the cotton beneath me.

'I really thought we'd actually be sleeping on a couch,' I said.

'I'm going to keep that to myself and enjoy the bed,' Hetty replied, yawning at the end. I heard her shuffle off her shoes, their plonk against the carpet, as I yawned back.

I lay on my temporary bed and felt myself fall into something just above dreams. I tried to think back to whether I had told Jo where we were from, whether she had known before we arrived that we were Australian. For some reason her lack of clarity made getting my footing here seem further away. I couldn't recall our email exchange, and then I was sleeping.

~

We woke early the next morning after a stop-start sleep and crept around the kitchen trying to find a way to make coffee, until Jo came down in a short red dressing gown and fluffy slippers.

'I'm an early riser,' she told us, reaching up for something in the pantry and showing us her undies. 'John sleeps as much as he possibly can, like a big old hibernating bear, even in summer!'

Jo laughed at this and I heard that when she laughed it sounded as if she was choking slightly and that it went on and on. So nervous was her laugh, and her presence in the kitchen, that I realised we would have to find somewhere to live pretty quickly, or I wouldn't be able to keep laughing when she laughed and would end up offending her.

'We're going to go for a walk. Might see you later?' I said, looking at Hetty as I did to try to make sure she didn't ask Jo along.

Jo's eyebrows knitted briefly, then she smiled, wishing us well, and suggesting we move towards one of the other neighbourhoods so we could start to understand Toronto. I had a map I'd printed back in Melbourne in my pocket, and I patted my jeans and pulled Hetty out the door.

On the street it was brisk and bright, and there were people walking by the apartment building in parkas with fluffy hoods. I didn't have a winter coat and was wearing five layers of jumper. Hetty had a duffel that she'd put on over a skivvy.

We stood and looked at each other. Hetty was smiling and I felt something winged soar up towards my throat.

'Where do you want to go first?' I asked her.

She moved to my side and looped her arm through the circle of mine.

'Wherever you think we should go, Nessy.'

I could see from my map that the area we were staying in was called the Financial District. Above us and to the left was a very tall tower with a bulb and a spike at its top. The map told me this was the CN Tower, from which you could see everything, and eat a tourist dinner. The people walking by in their parkas were carrying briefcases or shiny handbags, and had heels or dress pants on under the puff, but the buildings weren't as high as they could have been. It looked as if we could walk away from here and quickly be in other parts of the city.

Parkdale was straight ahead in one direction, and I wanted to see how different it was to the Parkdale on the outskirts of Melbourne—a broad, flat place of houses and car parks. As we walked, Hetty's step a little longer than mine so that I had to move fast, I watched the breath from people's mouths like tiny parts of them escaping, and remembered: *these people are Canadian.* It seemed strange that we were here, among them.

'We're in Canada,' I said, and nudged Hetty's ribs with my elbow. 'Canada!'

'And so far it looks quite a lot like Melbourne.' She laughed.

I agreed. I saw a broad, calm, halcyon city with buildings of various heights, mostly pale and wet from the damp wind. I looked up again, this time to the clouds, and couldn't see any. Instead there was a sort of white smoke against a grey blue. I hoped there would be clouds later in the day: white, slow, bloated ones that I could linger on.

I pictured what we might look like to those who passed

us—a tall girl in a maroon duffle coat a little too small for her, her long arms pulling at the skivvy underneath to keep her fingers warm, and her smaller friend with hair like a black scribble and some kind of body beneath all the layers, walking at a pace that suited neither, almost limping, almost falling. We were still only worth a quick, half-curious glance. I was happy with that.

I decided to keep the map in my pocket for a while and walk without knowing where, heading west. We popped up onto Queen Street, a wide thoroughfare with red trams running along its middle, and confident shops playing music.

'This is great,' Hetty breathed.

I pointed at a pile of dirty soft ice that sat beside the open door of an Urban Outfitters store, where a tall, broad bodyguard stood, eyes forward, back straight. We stopped to inspect it.

'So that's what snow becomes.'

We had talked about snow so much before we'd arrived that it seemed strange to have our first sighting outside an Urban Outfitters in April, when it was more of a brown mess than a white carpet. I had never imagined where the snow might go when the weather turned. Apparently it didn't go anywhere for quite a while, and the city kept on moving around it so that it lost its clarity and its power, and became just like everything else.

'Snow without make-up,' I said, to make Hetty laugh. She made a noise like a seal, and rubbed her arms.

'I still think it's beautiful,' she said.

'Of course you do, Het,' I said, rolling my eyes. 'Of course you do.'

I slipped my arm through hers to keep us moving.

We giggled our way down Queen Street past a vast park and restaurant after restaurant, until we turned and began a slow walk up the incline of a street called Ossington. There were a few Vietnamese cafes dotted between stores that seemed to sell clothes no one would wear, and an ice-cream place with a line, despite the hour and the chill. We kept walking up and found a little bakery with plastic chairs inside, and piles of sweet pastries and bready things that looked both familiar and different at once. It was a Portuguese bakery—said so in big red capital letters above the narrow eave.

Inside it was warm and doughy and the few customers looked as if they had been sitting there forever, baked and sweetened by their surroundings. A large woman with a small chest and floury hands greeted us at the counter. Hetty chose a cupcake-shaped parcel called an empada de pato. I picked a tiny bacon pudding and a slice of honey cake. There was sugar-donut dust on our table, and before we sat the woman came to wipe it off. She told us where the bathroom was, though we hadn't asked, and placed a large key between us. After we'd finished eating, Hetty told me she had never tasted anything so delicious, and thanked the woman over and over until we were out the door and on the street again, our mouths slick with fat.

'Let's go down to the water?' Hetty asked.

Hetty loved water, and had already told me all about Lake Ontario: how it was so big you couldn't see what lay on the other side; how, despite this, it was the smallest of the Great Lakes, and the most polluted, because its sister and brother lakes swam into it, and brought their mess with them. She'd read so much about it before we left that she'd become obsessed, and would talk to me about how she imagined we would love it, how it wasn't like the ocean but was still big and wide and cold, and how she wondered what it would be like to swim in it.

We started walking until we were back near where we had started on Spadina Avenue, having moved the opposite way along the broadness of Queen, and could soon see the greeny blue of Lake Ontario a little below. Toronto dipped down towards the water, and the wind I felt on my face was now connected to the texture I could see in the distance.

I'd never really thought about why Hetty loved water so much. She would lie in the bath for hours when we lived together in a one-bedroom flat in Brunswick above a charcoal-chicken shop, filling it up with a little more hot every so often, wiping her wet, wrinkled fingers on a towel to turn the dry pages of her book. I'd brush my teeth, do a wee, swish mouthwash at the sink while she lay there. She always looked serene, and so skinny. Hetty would rather swim in the ocean or run out into the rain or do laps of the local swimming pool than anything else. When it was stormy I would find her staring out at the puddles forming, the sky fountain. I wondered if someone who usually stood just above the world found it easier to move in water.

The wind got higher and swooped at us as we crossed the last road before the Harbourfront. There were people enjoying themselves down here, or trying to despite the weather. Hetty pulled me towards the edge of the walkway where there was a man selling tiny coloured flags on long sticks among little kids and dogs chasing each other. It didn't smell like salt but the air was wet: a pleasing, fresh kind of wet that helped me remember I was breathing.

We stood at the edge of the short stone wall and watched out over the blue and green and black water that moved gently, like a sleeping animal. Hetty inhaled deeply and moved closer to me, putting her silky head on my shoulder.

'It must be the ocean. It feels like it is,' she said softly, sleepily, as though she had just woken up.

'If you say it's the ocean, then it is,' I replied.

'It's the ocean,' she said, and lifted her head up to smile at me.

We stood there a long time looking out at the lake, trying to see something beyond the water. We stood until the sound of the children and animals around us died down to nothing, their small and pretty Canadian noises just wind. I shivered inside my jumpers and stood in the moment.

CHANNEL
especially two seas

Hetty and I met in Grade Two. It was the start of the year, and she had moved from another school in another suburb to be in my class, with Mrs Harris as our teacher. Mrs Harris was a strange woman—I could understand that even as a seven-year-old. She had tight brown curled hair that sat stiff around her head, a tanned face with slack pillow cheeks and nostrils that flared unpredictably, like a horse's. She didn't change her manner according to who she was talking to—she spoke to her pupils in the same blunt, flat way she spoke to my parents when they came to see the classroom, and the principal when he popped in to see how we all were. The principal was a man called Terry Hooven. He told all of us to call him Terry, and seemed to like us—the children—as well as the adults. He was thin, light on his feet, excitable. Mrs Harris stagnated beside him.

I hadn't really noticed Hetty until one day early in the year when it was raining terribly—the kind of rain that would almost scare you, when you would wonder if sheer water could take the earth away—and I was sitting at the window at recess, looking out. I was thinking about my four little guinea pigs, already with their vulnerable, delicate hearts, sitting in our backyard in their cage in the storm, shaking and making tiny, terrified peeping noises. I was on the verge of crying when I heard Hetty beside me say, 'Are you all right?'

Looking back, it seems unusual for one seven-year-old to ask after the wellbeing of another, but that was Hetty. She had five brothers and sisters and was born near the middle, and this had given her the strong sense at a young age that she was just one human among many.

Hetty had only ever told me a little about what it was really like in her house when she was growing up. She never said anything bad about her dad, but it became clear that he was sick with alcohol most of the time, and depressed the rest, and that he favoured some of his kids over the others. Hetty was a favourite, though I don't think she realised it. She never thought she was special, but she was. Even Mrs Harris sensed it, and gave her extra, unique tasks throughout the year, believing in her more than she did the rest of us, with our snotty noses and claggy paws. The only time I saw Mrs Harris move her heavy mouth up into a smile was when she was talking to Hetty.

That rainy day was ours. I told Hetty I was worried for my four little guinea friends, and she confided in me that she was worried for her two rabbits, also outside in her backyard in a flimsy hutch—all those tiny animals at one with the thunder and lightning and sheets of water. We sat together and talked about how we hoped they were safe, convincing each other that our animals were stronger than they were. We grabbed for each other's hands when the thunder got louder, and when recess ended we sat together for the rest of the day. I didn't have siblings—just a worn-out mother and a silent father—and I was lonely. I sometimes wonder if Hetty had sensed from that first day how much I needed her.

From then on we were firm friends, and I began to understand the ways Hetty could help me, with her gentle laugh and imagination and sweeping care for everything. Through primary school and high school she stayed close by me, even when she became much more popular, much more admired than me, and when she was confirmed to be very beautiful. Loyalty suited her: I saw how the other kids started to see me as cool simply because she behaved as if I mattered. I let their eyes dally on me and was thankful.

Hetty and I had made a sort of pact when we were sixteen that we would travel together to the other side of the world one day and live there for as long as we could brave it, in order to become better, more alive versions of ourselves. We knew that Melbourne was so far from the parts of the world that seemed to really matter, and that the drear of suburban Ringwood, where we had spent our days circling, trying to find something, was even farther. We didn't leave when we had planned to, because Hetty fell in love with a guy called Sean just after we finished high school, and he ruined her life for a while, or at least stopped her from considering university or reaching out beyond herself to find out who she could be.

Sean was obsessed with Hetty, and became more and more frightened that she would leave him. I was clearly a threat, and he was snarling at me rather than talking by the time it ended, telling Hetty I was a bitch when I was in the next room of their two-bedroom flat in Reservoir, calling their pet kelpie after me to make sure I knew he thought I was a dog. Hetty was so sorry for everything Sean did—from the beginning he placed her in anxious debt to everyone around them—but he knew how to make her feel for him, and how to pull her in with the tentacles he grew over those four long years.

When Hetty was finally able to leave him, I wanted us to fly to Toronto straight away, to move beyond the pain she was feeling and the risk of her closing in on herself for good, but it took another whole year of Hetty and Sean bumping up against each other before she was able to truly pull herself free. He killed himself two days after she told him she couldn't talk to him anymore, leaving a note that said she was heartless and had left him unable to live.

Hetty broke into pieces then, and moved into my place, where she didn't go to work or eat or cry or smile, spending her time lying in bed facing the wall or trudging off on long, aimless walks that she came back from gaunt and blank. I didn't really know how to talk to her about what had happened—I hated Sean so much I couldn't hear her speak of him with grace and love, and my anger meant she backed off from my pleas to let the guilt go. We kept smiling at each other, but her smiles were small and polite, and I felt our friendship dying.

It was only after a long summer that Hetty spent by herself near water—the Yarra River, Red Bluff beach, the dam on her uncle's property in Kangaroo Ground—and months of me leaving her alone even when I wanted to ask her everything, that she came back, and we booked our flights to Canada.

OASIS
a fertile spot in a desert, where water is found

We found a place to live after a fortnight in Jo and John's spare room, and it was freedom to leave, a freedom I had expected to feel the moment we arrived but hadn't, perhaps due to jet lag, or because expectation often leads to disappointment. In that two weeks we had scouted some of the city and had decided where we liked and could see ourselves living.

Despite his calm presence, John had been impossible to get to know, and would either sit silently on the couch or retreat upstairs each night. It was Jo who Hetty and I became unexpectedly fond of—she tried so hard it was impossible not to want to help her along. And she did listen, once she got past the obvious urge she had to tell her part. We spoke about her late into some nights, fascinated by her bubbles, her spiked energy and the blatant sadness she was fighting to ignore. Hetty admitted first that she had begun to like Jo, that she might even hope that we kept in touch. As was Hetty's way, she pioneered tenderness and helped me feel it too.

'I'll miss you two!' Jo said into my hair as she hugged me goodbye the day we left.

'We'll miss you too, Jo,' Hetty said, and we promised to see each other again.

From Jo and John's to our new place wasn't far and we only had our packs, so we walked. It was a beautiful morning—the sky was bright and there was sun across everything, but the air on our faces was cold. People were moving slowly; it was a Saturday, and we were in the part of Toronto that was mostly office buildings, so it wasn't crowded. The old, slow red trams moved up and down collecting slow people. I couldn't call them streetcars yet.

We were moving into a big share house in Chinatown, on a street off Spadina Avenue. Hetty had seen it without me—I had been sleeping when she found the ad online, so she wandered up on her own, saw the room and met the five housemates we would be living with. She told me when she got home that it was 'messy' and 'perfect'.

We walked along slowly with our packs on our backs, beyond Queen Street and up Spadina. There were all sorts of people around us: a large man with a sign pretending to sell rugs on the corner, his guitar case open for anyone who wanted to throw him some coins; teenagers outside McDonald's with large Cokes; women huddled in groups selling bamboo and aloe and mint leaves.

When we got to the house, down a leafy street off the main, Hetty said, 'This is it,' and I looked up and saw how tall it was. Three storeys, with windows all over and grand steps leading up to the front door and verandah. It looked like a house out of a movie, with a family and a basement and a big, soft dog.

Hetty rang the doorbell and we waited, pulling our packs off for relief. There was a small wooden sign next to the front door that read MARJORIE in curled letters. I had never lived in a house with a name. It seemed old-fashioned and charming.

The door was answered by a pretty girl with mouse-blond hair and a tattoo like a vine circling her neck. She told me her name was Ingrid, and smiled so I could see her small white teeth. I put out my hand to shake hers and felt it flat and warm in mine. We were welcomed inside, where it smelt like sandalwood and cooked onions. A quiet cat wound around my legs.

Steph, Ingrid, Dill, Clark and Robin. Two girls, three boys, one cat called Whitney. They told us when I bent down to pat her that her name had been Puss until the day after Whitney Houston died, when Puss retreated to her spot under Dill's bed for three days, seemingly grieving, and they decided she should be called Whitney. They laughed at this, and so did Hetty. I found it hard to keep up with things when I was nervous and my laugh came slightly after, echoing a little in the honey-floorboarded kitchen. Whitney nuzzled at my legs as if to say: Don't worry. Everyone smiled and seemed kind.

Dill helped us lift our bags up the two flights of stairs to our bedroom. He was chatty in in a reassuring way, as if he would like you no matter what, and he had soft brown hair and long eyelashes. Hetty bit her lip, her eyes straight ahead as we followed him. I noticed when Hetty's face changed: she was squishing up her nose and her mouth and her cheeks a bit when he spoke to her, as if it was scary to let him really see.

We waited until he had set our bags down in the middle of the room before we went in. It was dusty and bright, with a big window and a big bed and holes in the paint where the posters of the last housemate must have been stuck up with Blu Tack. Whitney had followed us, and jumped up to circle the mattress and knead at the fabric. Her purring made my cheeks warm, and Dill and Hetty smiled and looked at each other and the floor until Dill said he would leave us, and he did, and we sat down on our packs and said nothing together for a while.

~

The house thrummed. I'd never lived somewhere where people cared for each other so much, and concentrated earnestly on the best things about being young and alive. Hetty had always been my window into this sort of thing, even though sometimes her eyes clouded over and she couldn't see anything much at all. Now I was living in a space that was fuelled by an energy I'd never had. I was shy around it, and only started to feel close to comfortable after I had been alone in Marjorie a few times—after I'd had a chance to wander around without worrying who I would bump into and what I would say.

The day after we arrived, Hetty set out and got herself a job at a bar in Kensington Market. It was a dark place with two beers on tap and cheap spirits and house wine from a box, and there was a shop across the street that made hot greasy grilled-cheese sandwiches for the drinkers who had started early and needed food. Ronnie's seemed iconic in that way that meant it would never change. The chairs were odd and broken, the toilets were sticky and smelly, and people came to drink there at lunchtime and stayed until close. I felt intimidated when I walked in, but Hetty suited it. She was angled the right way for something cool, and too dreamy to know it.

Hetty was there a lot those first few weeks and needed to sleep when she wasn't, so I walked around alone each day trying to find somewhere I thought I could see myself working, looking up at things and counting the weird dogs everyone seemed to have with them on brightly coloured leashes. It was the beginning of May by then, the weather was warming up and on my own I got to know how beautiful spring could be in Toronto. Trinity Bellwoods was bare one day and when I came back the next, flowers had bloomed everywhere. They grew where no one had planted them, like our russet-coloured ones back home, but they were blue and purple and pink, like lollies.

I walked all the way to High Park one morning, huffing along in a parka until I had to take it off and tie it around my waist. I had never been in such a beautiful park—it was impossible not to get lost, because it was so wild and thick, and there were hills and large neat green spaces and thickets where dogs were allowed to jump and run. I wished so much that Hetty was there; it seemed less special on my own, though I was trying hard to be happy and in the moment and free, like everyone around me seemed to be.

I sat down on a bench in the middle of nowhere—tall thin fresh trees standing all around, and a damp forest floor—and had a little cry. I was glad I was there, in High Park, in Toronto. It wasn't that. It was just hard sometimes to keep smiling, to keep moving and looking and trying, when you sensed you were being left behind.

One night I was in our room in bed early, trying to sleep, when someone knocked quietly on the door.

'Ness, are you there?' It sounded like Steph, who had a voice that was dry and close. 'We're having drinks downstairs if you're awake.'

I loved how the Canadian accent came out gently, no matter who was speaking. It was easy to say yes, to say no, to a voice that didn't ask anything of you. In Australia I avoided conversation to avoid the commitment that came with it. Here, I felt more like I could speak. I sat up and said I was coming.

In the living room there were bodies lying or sitting on every bit of comfortable space. I was handed a mug of wine by Robin, who was wearing a pretty cardigan that looked like it was made out of lichen or wool mist, if there were such a thing. I reached out to touch it, then asked if I could, the wrong way around. He laughed and rubbed the sleeve against my cheek.

Robin was so beautiful he seemed to glow when he walked into the kitchen in his pyjamas in the morning or when you came upon him in the hallway. He was the only one of us other than Dill who could pick up Whitney—I had tried every day since we had moved in, and she was only now starting to let me tug and scratch at the soft hair behind her ears. Robin had pale hair and pale skin and pale eyes and thick, dark eyebrows that moved more than the rest of him did. He touched and kissed often, and never interrupted, only speaking after he had waited and heard properly what the other person was saying. His careful attention made me feel a little anxious, though I wished that it didn't.

'Were you sleeping?' he asked, smiling and watching me.

'Just resting,' I answered.

He pulled me down to sit next to him on one of the big green couches. It sank low, and smelt like moss. Everyone seemed to be talking at once. I took a gulp of the wine, which was sweet and cold. It travelled through me, lighting up parts along the way. I could see Hetty wasn't here, and for once I was glad. Maybe I could forge my own friendship with the house and all the people that visited it so often. It was tiring to need Hetty by my side. Especially now that she was so often nowhere near me.

I sat and listened to the voices of everyone—all different but all with the same lilt. It seemed like I might be able to sit without talking for a while. It was nice to be warm and down deep with the fabric all around and voices keeping me company. There were people I had seen and met before, and others I hadn't.

A very attractive girl with long, tangled ash-blond hair was sitting on the floor opposite me. When she laughed I noticed she had a gold tooth, nestled back behind her front ones, and that she was a little too on, like a supermarket bulb. I watched her until she looked over at me, probably feeling the heat of my eyes on her face, and then I pretended I was lost in thought. I was looking at the edge of someone else when I heard a voice ring out above the others. I looked over and saw the gold-toothed girl looking straight at me, her eyes hard and clear.

'Are you Ness?'

I nodded, after a little while, and tried to smile. Sometimes when I was nervous and I tried to say something or move my face it was as if the corners of my mouth were being pulled back and forth, up and down by an invisible string, like I was a puppet and someone else controlled me. I held my hand up and a little bit over my face and looked back, trying to sit larger against the sagging foam.

'Where's Hetty, then?' the girl asked.

Someone laughed, then someone else. I couldn't tell if everyone had stopped talking and the laughing was because of me and Hetty and because it was embarrassing that I was never apart from her because I relied on her so much and needed her even though she didn't need me.

Robin touched my leg and looked over at the girl, who was taking a long drink from a tall beer can.

'Hetty's not here, Sylvie. Ness is our favourite, anyway.'

I smiled with embarrassment at how untrue that must have been, and Robin scooted an arm around my waist and leaned in, whispering hot in my ear. 'Ignore her. Sylvie loves being a bitch.'

Sylvie, was all I could think. Sylvie. It was a beautiful name. Hetty wouldn't like her, but wouldn't say she didn't. It would be one of those times her nose would wrinkle up, pleats appearing on either side of the length of it. No narrow words, no heated opinion. Just that disapproving nose. I heard words again around me that I didn't need to make sense of and felt Robin next to me, his voice responding slowly to questions and suggestions. The wine warmed against my leg. I let the voices fade.

WASH
the water disturbed by a moving boat

One morning I was lying in bed on my side, my eyes slightly open, watching the leaves of the Norway maple outside our window shimmer with green and sun. Hetty stirred next to me, sat straight up and yawned. She looked down and shook me a little with both hands, leaning in to whisper in my ear, 'Let's go to the islands.'

Her breath was cosy against my face and I was tired, but I sat up straight too and smiled. I'd been so scared that she had stopped wanting to do things together, just the two of us: that our time had passed again.

The Toronto Islands were close to the mainland—a few bits of land that had dropped from the mouth and been forgotten about. You could get there on a small ferry that didn't take very long, and we had heard there were houses there and pretend beaches, places where people sunbathed nude and drank tallboys of beer on blankets. As we walked down Spadina, down the hill that eventually led to the dock, Hetty told me what she knew about the various islands already, facts from the people she worked with mixed with things she had read when she googled behind the bar at night.

'People live on the islands—Torontonians, or Toronto Islanders maybe they're called? It's hard to get a house there, though. You can't buy one. You have to go into a ballot and then you get to rent.'

'That sounds ideal.'

'Yeah,' Hetty said. 'And it's pretty hippie over there—to live—I've heard. Like, you can't just have a pool and a four-wheel-drive and go waterskiing. You have to respect the culture that already exists.' She stopped to pull at her ponytail, taking out a bobby pin and putting it between her teeth while she tied her hair up again. 'It's nice.'

I could feel the wind coming off the water as we crossed over the bridge that stood above Lake Shore Boulevard and ducked through the bushes to walk along the bike path. The water of Lake Ontario shimmered in the near distance. Hetty was smiling when I looked over at her. I loved Toronto just then, and the feeling of being in a place where you lived but didn't come from, where you were essentially invisible. We could explore without having to be tourists, and pretend we were locals until we opened our mouths and spoke. We could live without the eyes of people who had known us a long time watching and waiting. I took Hetty's hand, curling each of my fingers around hers.

After we had bought our tickets at the terminal, Hetty said she wanted to sit near the water to wait for the ferry. To the side of the gates there was a little spot of grass and we lay down with our bags as pillows. There were so many noises—water splashing stoutly up against land, tyres on bitumen, children screaming, parents laughing and yelling and pleading. I wondered if it was school holidays but couldn't work out when they might be. The sky above was beautiful, with chubby clouds hanging in little groups as if they were talking to each other: little cliques of clouds and a sun in the middle that warmed my eyelashes. The clouds were prettier here. Even when it was grey the sky seemed perfect.

The honk of the ferry as it approached the dock was long and swollen. We stayed stretched out on the ground, then slowly gathered ourselves. If Hetty hadn't been there I would have been rushing. I didn't like to be late for things: arriving at the last minute after everyone else was settled twisted my insides. Hetty arrived whenever she did with a cute face saying sorry and such lazy grace that no one could blame her.

I picked up my duffel bag slowly, deliberately, to make sure the day was meditative and I would enjoy it. With Hetty there, hurry clotted and waned. She had always told me that I helped her see more clearly and remember what she needed to do and when. Maybe this was true, but my constant inner paddling dismayed me. Hetty was a piece of grass swaying lightly in any kind of wind. I couldn't deny that it felt like the happier way.

We decided to sit outside on the deck, to watch the water and let the wind mess our hair. There weren't many others coming with us: a few older women in walking boots with kerchiefs at their necks; a solemn young couple and their tiny dog; a family with two little children who were screaming, their small red hands held tight by the parents' larger ones.

There was a feeling moving through the air inside the ferry that I couldn't put my finger on—a sadness that didn't involve the heart. I was glad we were sitting outside with the view, and the green smell of lake water.

'I just can't make myself believe this isn't the sea,' Hetty said, leaning over the edge, her face raw. 'It looks like ocean water. It feels like it when it sprays up on my face.'

'You can't see the edge of it. That's the problem,' I answered, though it didn't really feel like a problem, but more of a curiosity, an odd fact.

'Oh well. It's a beautiful lake. A beautiful whatever-it-is.' Hetty spread her arms out a little in the hard air, and turned to grin at me.

As the ferry moved slowly across the water Hetty brought out a bottle of rum, the label eaten half away. She swigged and passed it to me and I followed, the liquid burning down my throat and into my chest like a tiny fire. The bottle was small and we shared the whole thing while Hetty told me about how she felt all sorts of things for Dill, but he didn't seem interested, and I disagreed and told her how his face moved forward and up and down more when she was there, and sometimes it froze, as if he wasn't sure quite what to do with it. I told Hetty how it felt funny to be in the room with the two of them, with so much heat, and how I reckoned he was actually obsessed with her, and who wouldn't be.

She laughed a little, and asked me if I was just saying that, and I told her I wasn't. I could feel the warmth in my chest fading at the thought of Hetty being in love with someone proper, someone kind and real, because that would really take her away from me. I resigned myself to trying to find someone of my own, someone else, while Hetty told me how she thought about having sex with Dill in the shower and wished he would walk in on her. Then we arrived, and stepped off the ferry, our faces flushed and our hair wild, and we were there on the islands.

I felt I should ask Hetty more about her plans for Dill, whether she was imagining they would become boyfriend and girlfriend. It seemed almost boring, to be with him, to settle into something, to be contented and slow, but I knew that was probably what she wanted. When I was little, my dad had often told me that I was 'determined to be miserable', and I had taken this very seriously. He must have known me best, my father, with his weak chin coated in bristles and his certain voice, because he saw how impossible I really was.

I didn't ask Hetty anything more. She let things go, Hetty; she didn't push conversations if she felt someone wasn't interested, and though I had never taken advantage of this part of her before, I did that day. It seemed like it would be exhausting to go over it any longer, and I had nothing helpful to offer her. I didn't know how she could find out if Dill liked her too, though I was pretty sure that he did, that he would have to, if she had shone her eyes in his direction. It wouldn't be helpful for her to ask me how to do it. Maybe I was burnt out from Sean, from the years of holding Hetty together when a man had pulled her apart. I knew Dill was nothing like Sean, but it didn't seem to matter.

~

A large white cat greeted us at the dock, despite appearing weary of visitors. I leaned down to ask if I could pat it and it sprang away, its big fluffy body moving quicker than I would have thought possible. It was colder here than on the mainland, and the air was slightly wet. We were on Ward's Island, the part where people lived, because Hetty wanted to see what the houses were like, and the people.

As we walked up the path towards some buildings that might have been public toilets or a community centre or a shop, I imagined what it would have been like to grow up in a place like this. It was quiet, and the air with its little droplets and occasional puffs of sharp was not like the air in Toronto. The cool seemed to be coming from a bigger sky with more clouds. As a child I would have cycled around here on a little bike, with my hippie island friends, and we would have been able to hide behind the bushes I could see, from our parents and our siblings, and our cats and dogs, and the mainlanders who would have been coming over for a peek, even back then.

I told Hetty I would have liked to have lived here as a child, and she agreed. We hadn't seen anything yet, but it felt a little bit special, with the silence and the green all around. The grey-haired women with their kerchiefs had stayed on the ferry for the next stop, as had the teenage couple and the harried family, their expressions making me determined I would never have kids. We were alone.

Hetty loved the houses. I watched her face as we walked down a sort of street near the water lined with one-storey brick veneers. Most were mute and earthy in their decoration, but one was loud and crowded with sculptures made of forks and a skull as a doorknocker. There was a tabby licking itself on the porch next to a looming Peruvian torch cactus in a black pot, and music coming from within, slightly too loud. That house seemed out of place, and I wondered how tolerant the islanders were to those who moved in and didn't maintain their home as well as the rest, or had different ideas and tastes.

I told Hetty there would be an older man somewhere behind those curtains, that brick, with long grey hair and collapsed cheeks from forgetting to eat. He would have won the Toronto Island lottery because he had entered when he was drunk, or as a joke, or because he was quietly insane and made tiny decisions that upheaved his existence all the time. He would talk in grunts that were barely audible, and would own no cats but feed hundreds of them.

Hetty laughed and nodded so much she fell sideways into one of the trees at the edge of his property, decorated with loops of FRAGILE tape, making me laugh and the cat get up and angrily meow at us to go away. I thought to myself that the old man's efforts were beautiful.

~

We walked a large part of the island that day, the wind in our ears telling us to move forward. Hetty wanted to get to the Gibraltar Point Lighthouse, which she had heard was made of crooked bricks and a bright-red door. The occasional person would pass us as we neared the end of the residential section—mostly older men or women with burnt cheeks and practical haircuts. We walked through what seemed to be an abandoned children's adventure park, then past a beautiful, clean area with a fountain and monuments and couples sitting on stone benches.

On the bushy road nearing Gibraltar we saw groups of teenagers and older hippies trailing along with dogs and blankets and bongs or guitars, one group wrapped up in their coats and carrying an old couch. I could feel that there was life behind the bushes, and I knew that would be where the edges of the island met the water of Lake Ontario.

At one point we dipped down through an opening in the foliage and a clear view of the water, and walked along the dirty sand. There were men there, lying or sitting on coloured towels, and some of them were naked. They were middle-aged, with pot-bellied stomachs and skinny, vulnerable legs, and when I saw the penis of one of them it looked so small and harmless I didn't feel anything. Hetty pulled at my arm and I looked at her face, which was big-eyed. She was mouthing *Sorry* but I shook my head and told her later she hadn't needed to be. It would have been like being upset about a worm.

We flopped on a bit of beach that was brown and crunchy, past the nudists and their quiet displays. I wanted to feel close to the environment, so while Hetty lay on the towel she had brought, I lay on the sand itself, picking up a handful and moving it between my thumb and my finger. I wondered why there was sand here, on the edge of a lake. Maybe it had travelled here with the ocean.

'Hey, Hetty, maybe you're right—I think you are right, actually. This *is* the ocean. There's sand and everything.'

I brought a handful up to my face and let it scatter. It felt cold and heavy against my closed eyes, skin.

'You always know how to make me feel better,' Hetty

replied. My eyes were still shut, and I was wondering how to open them without the sand getting in.

'It's so nice to hang out,' I heard her say, and I brushed the sand from my skin, feeling my heart beat a little faster. I opened my eyes and looked over.

Hetty was lying on her back on the towel, which she had brought with her from Melbourne, the one that I had seen her dry herself with after swimming since we were young. It was tattered around the edges but intact in a way it really shouldn't have been after so long. Her legs were bent, one crossed over the other, one skinny foot hanging free.

'I'm sorry I haven't been around much,' she said.

I told her it was okay. It was okay, now that she had acknowledged that it wasn't really. That was all I needed. I was partly weak, partly docile, partly aware of how much I still needed her. She wouldn't be pushed away easily, but I didn't want to try. I believed we had decided to come to Canada together because we were both invested in our friendship, despite my feelings which she knew nothing about, and that since we had been here she had neglected it. I also knew that it wasn't deliberate, this neglect: it wasn't purposeful.

'How are you, anyway?' she asked, studying my face for a few seconds. When Hetty looked at you, it was like she was right there with you—like you weren't alone.

'I'm fine!' I answered, in a voice she could have questioned for its quaver.

'Good,' she said, smiling at me as if she believed it. 'That's so good to hear.'

Later I would wonder what it would be like if Hetty and I

had a different kind of friendship, or if we were different people: the kind who laid it all out and hoped for the best. I had been hurt and I hadn't been okay—not really. But I didn't tell her. I didn't want to ask more of her, to tie her down. And I didn't want a reaction. Instead we questioned, gently, her first and then me, and didn't try to tether each other. It suited us both, suited our passivity and our fear. But our friendship hadn't grown in years.

We ended the day silently, on the ferry back to Marjorie, our hair damp from a long swim in the lake water. Hetty held my hand occasionally and put her chin and then her ear on my shoulder as the water moved beneath us. I could feel her hanging on. We both wanted to be each other's person, but our bodies were moving apart. She seemed to need me to know it was just a brief change in the current.

RIP
cutting through the lines of breaking waves like a river running out to sea

I got a job at a small, strange cafe across the road from the crystal-ship building of the Art Gallery of Ontario. It was called Cafe Art Song, and was trying to be a place that hung paintings, where people would come and play music, as well as one that served food and drink from a comprehensive menu—sixty-five dishes and fifty different beverages to choose from. It was both overwhelming and underwhelming when I first walked in, and daggy enough for me to feel I could ask about a job without the usual sense of inadequacy.

They said I could work as much as I wanted. The owner was a tall, cold white guy called Sim who was never there, and my direct supervisor was a tiny woman called Minnie, who seemed never to leave. I couldn't work out if they were lovers, or a forever-married couple, or whether Minnie was just the kind of person who devoted herself to whatever she was doing and they were merely colleagues with a common interest—the success of this funny place. It didn't really matter. It was warm and quiet, and I needed money, occupation, distraction: something to make it feel like I was moving again.

The first few weeks I worked every day, and it quickly became a happy time to walk from our big, messy house up along the lather of Spadina and then right onto Dundas Street, letting the warming air remind me it was nearly summer. We had been in Toronto for two months, and I loved the organised grit of the area where we lived and worked.

Customers came into Cafe Art Song in trickles, but we kept ourselves busy turning paper napkins into origami swans, and telling each other where we had come from and how we felt about it. Minnie's parents were Korean, and though she had been born in Canada she told me she felt confused inside—as if she might never feel right in either place, Korea or Canada. The food she cooked for me and the few customers each lunchtime was so fierce and delicate, I wanted Hetty to try it. There was always a small bowl filled with kimchi beside the plate and I ate it slowly, concentrating on the shouty red of it and the bubbles I imagined on my tongue. I pushed out each small thought that came while I sat and ate, and tried to just enjoy.

One morning Minnie and I were sitting out the front because there was a slip of sun we wanted to catch. It was sugar weather—warmer days but still-cold nights—and somewhere near us sap would be starting to flow from the maple trees. Minnie had made us tall glasses of sweet thick milk and whipped cream so we could pretend we were customers to attract real customers, and we were talking about Australia. Minnie had heard that there were spiders everywhere there, and I was confirming this with a story about the huntsman that had dropped on my head when I was small. She was aghast at the name 'huntsman', I could barely believe she had never heard it before, and I was explaining that not all spiders dropped but that these ones did sometimes. All of a sudden, moving through the burning sun was tall Hetty, and after she bent down to hug me I couldn't grasp what I should say. I had forgotten she even knew where I was working, and she had a friend in tow who looked sharp and pointy, like an arrow.

'Hi, I'm Ness,' I said finally, standing up and holding out my hand to the girl.

'Hi,' she replied, hands untouchable in her jeans pockets.

Hetty told me her friend's name was Elaine, which sounded old-fashioned and separate from this barbed person standing defiant on the concrete, sun in her eyes and no hand up for shade. I'd never heard of Elaine, but I hadn't said much to Hetty in weeks—had just listened to her slow breath in the dark next to me after she crawled into bed each night and quickly fell asleep. I told Hetty that Minnie was Minnie and told Minnie that Hetty was Hetty, and they smiled at each other. I was glad to see Hetty, my body suddenly warmer near hers.

She said they'd come to see me, so they sat on two of the plastic chairs and Minnie went inside to make them sticky milk drinks. I told them they should eat too, wanting to say everything good to Hetty about Minnie's cooking but worrying Elaine would think me tedious, or artless in my praise. Hetty said she wasn't hungry and I watched her arms move towards her glasses, the fabric of the jumper hanging over the skinny of her.

Elaine only seemed to look at me when I wasn't looking at her and every time I tried to catch her eyes they darted back and forth, like a squirrel. She didn't smile at any of my half-jokes, though I knew that they weren't actually funny. She seemed like the type of person who was scornful of sincerity, and back then that was all I had.

'Remind me how you two met?' I asked. I could pretend I knew what was going on in Hetty's life and her head if I told myself I already knew that she had a new person.

Elaine still didn't look at me, but uncrossed her legs and sat forward a little, moving her eyes up from the ground towards Hetty. I wondered if she was blinking more slowly than people usually blink, or if it was just that tense calm some people had, as if they were daring you to bother. I noticed that she had scars on the inside of her arm near her elbow pit. They were long and white and thick.

'I'm Hetty's manager,' Elaine said. She didn't smile, or move her face at all. 'At Ronnie's.'

'Oh, cool! And you guys became friends? That's great.'

Elaine finally looked at me. Her eyes were black holes edged with black eyeshadow and short, thick black eyelashes. She didn't reply.

I glanced at Hetty, who was grinning at me in that worried way she sometimes did. I picked up my milk and took a long sip through the straw, a sweet waterfall down my throat. I disliked Elaine so much already, I didn't know how long I could sit there. I couldn't be rude back, not in the way she was to me: so carelessly, slightly, as if I didn't exist. I remembered that I was at work, that I would or should have to go back and do something soon anyway. Hetty couldn't expect me to stop my shift and speak to her just because she'd finally thought to come by and say hello. She was so fluffy sometimes.

'That's a Frank Gehry, you know,' Elaine said, nodding her head at the gallery, where it stood like a big dry ship, beautiful, like it was every day. I hadn't been inside yet. I'd kept telling myself that I'd go in after work one day and wander around, but it had never actually happened after my shift was over and my hands smelt like sweet flour and my feet were sore from standing.

We watched the building. It was golden and full of windows and I wanted to live in there. I felt like that every time I looked at it. I wished I had known the name of the architect, known that he was worth mentioning. I would google Frank Gehry when I got home.

I stood up and picked up my milk glass and Minnie's. She hadn't come back out after she had set down the two tall glasses of froth on the table for Hetty and Elaine. I suddenly wanted only to be inside helping her.

'I'd better get back to work, anyway,' I said, looking at Hetty and not at Elaine.

'Oh, of course—yes—of course,' Hetty answered, her eyes pleading with me or maybe just wild with fatigue and a lack of something, perhaps safety, which I couldn't help her with right now.

'Thanks for coming to visit!' I said, grabbing her hand to squeeze it. It was cold, and felt like recycled paper. I started to walk down the steps towards the cafe and waved.

'Later,' Elaine said, but I didn't look over and I didn't reply.

I was sick of being friendly, and of the reminder that one nice thing once in a while was not enough anymore—never had been, though I had pretended for so long. I hoped Hetty would come again without her.

DAM
a dam is a barrier

Since we were young, Hetty had been the one people looked at. Men, women, other children. She captivated them, and I saw that once they were captivated they didn't want to lose her. This fear of loss sometimes resulted in strange behaviour—girls at school following her around at lunchtime, day after day, as if in a trance; the man behind the counter at the milk bar lost for words whenever she came with me to buy a dollar's worth of bananas and teeth; my father staring at her and then asking her question after question in our kitchen on the rare times she came to my house, his eyes following her as she moved around, waiting for her glass of orange juice.

I was never jealous, because I didn't expect that kind of adoration. The way I looked didn't capture anyone, and no one seemed to feel the need to let their eyes linger on me, or tell me how impressed they were by my height or my hair or my face. I could see, like everyone else, that Hetty had beauty. I wasn't jealous, because I was captivated too.

There is a memory that sticks with me, that I come back to sometimes, of Hetty and me as girls. The memory is of a day about five years after we had met, at a time when our friendship was close and innocent. We were twelve and it was the summer holidays, with many long, languid afternoons stretched out in front of us like a horizon. There is a blurred edge to the memory, and I am unsure why. When I asked Hetty about it over the years, she told me she remembered very little of the day, and seemed to have nothing at all to say about it. I still don't know whether she had repressed the details, or couldn't tell me the truth.

We had pleaded with our parents—my mother, Hetty's father; both difficult to convince for different reasons—to let us spend the day at Hetty's uncle Tom's property in Kangaroo Ground while he was away, and they had agreed, with the proviso that we wear our hats, clean up after ourselves and not swim in the dam. I had realised by this point that parents were terrified of water, of children drowning, of floods and disease, and though we both knew how to swim, Tom's dam was wide, and deep in the middle. When I had asked my mother if I could go, I saw her anxiety bring her there, to the middle of that dam, where I would flail and start swallowing water, despite my years of swimming lessons and the fact that I never put my body in danger. Hetty's father was also protective, but in a more extravagant, aggressive way. He had told her he would kill her if she went swimming, though we all knew she would do it, and the threat hung above us that morning after we were left there on our own.

We spent the morning in Tom's shack. It was dark inside,

with wooden floors and walls and a kindling ceiling, a ruffled bed shy in one corner of the only room. There was a strong smell of must, though it faded quickly, and reminded me of the smell of my sleeping bag after months rolled up and packed away for winter. The only photos on display were of Tom's sister's family—Hetty's mother and Hetty's siblings and Hetty. They all watched us from frames above the fireplace. I asked Hetty to tell me about her uncle, curious to find out about this man who didn't seem to inhabit much of his own life.

'He has depression,' she said, carefully. 'He gets really sick sometimes. But then sometimes he's okay.'

I knew about depression—my mother had it. My father had used the word only once but it had stuck, and back then I ascribed all of her behaviour to that word, without nuance or understanding. With my mother, the depression was a blanket that covered her entirely, that I lifted when I could find the edge, and that she told me was too warm or too cold, depending on the day. With Tom, I imagined it to be even more impenetrable, like a splintered piece of wood stuck fast in his chest across his heart.

When Hetty showed me the only photo he was in, I could see he was tall and young, at least younger than the other adults in my life. I liked him and I liked his tiny house that didn't seem to be the way most people thought a house should be. Hetty seemed to like him too.

We cooked a sort of lunch on Tom's stove. I can't remember what it was, that meal, but I remember there were only two aluminium plates in the cupboard and one sharp knife. I remember we ate with our hands, licking each finger clean, and that we enjoyed it. I ate more than Hetty, I'm sure; she never had much of an appetite and hated to feel too full, as if the stretch against her stomach was dangerous. We gulped down tepid water from Tom's tap, Hetty reminding me to drink more than I wanted, to keep my body wet. It was a warm day, and hot inside Tom's shack, with its steel roof. We changed into our bathers in separate corners, me sneaking a glimpse of Hetty as I bent to pick up my undies, knowing even then that her back was more beautiful to me than mine would ever be to her.

There was no question of not swimming. Down by the dam I threw my towel up above me so that it billowed and let it spread out against the red ground. It was both dusty and sticky there, near the edge, but I didn't care if my things got dirty. I wanted to be cool and free, so I took off my T-shirt and sat down in my old bathers on the towel, feeling the fabric creep up in between my legs because they were too small and I needed new ones and it hadn't seemed important until right then.

I wanted to watch Hetty's body as she waded, so I urged her to go first and she did, so freely, making little bird noises as the water swallowed her. I found her beautiful and too perfect, but that day it didn't feel painful. Soon after, I joined her, and we both grew brave enough to sink right into the water and swim around in the caramel colour of it. I don't remember if it was cold but I imagine it must have been. I know the afternoon sky grew dull before we came out again, Hetty long after me because she was a water baby.

At some point I needed to go to the toilet. Tom only had an

outhouse that sat far away from both the dam and the shack, over where the smell of it would only disturb the kangaroos and the skinks, under a dying yellow box. I told Hetty I was going and she answered with her eyes closed, lying back on her towel to soak in the sun. Her hair was even longer back then, and in its half-dry state it looked like seaweed soon after it has beached itself: dark and thick with previous life. I saw how the curve of her hip was round in a way that no boy's body or man's body was. I knew briefly that that was what I wanted, then let the knowing go.

~

My walk to the toilet and back took longer than it should have. I was barefoot, and careful to avoid the burrs and the ants, of which there were many. I sat long on the toilet and sang a song to myself: I remember that because a bird outside the outhouse seemed to be singing along, until I stopped and it kept warbling. After I had scooped in the right amount of sawdust from a bucket near the door, I opened and closed the door of the outhouse carefully and looked for the bird that had been singing in the big tree above. There was no movement and no feathers that I could see, but as I turned to walk back towards Hetty and the dam, there was movement and a rustle in the grass near me, and I stopped still to see what it was.

More rustles revealed the small spiked body and thin snout of an echidna, making its way along, trying to find a snack. I watched the way it moved, precisely and with great purpose, snuffling at the earth for ants, safe in the knowledge that it was covered in spiky armour. It didn't appear to notice me, but I wondered if that was an echidna's way—to appear unruffled in order to stay that way. I watched it a while, backing carefully away as it neared me so I wouldn't frighten it; then it turned and started to move in another direction. I realised that I was hot and should get back to Hetty.

I turned and began walking back towards the dam, seeing then that there were two bodies there now, and that they were close together. My feet sped up before I could register the sight. I had left her, where we weren't even supposed to be, down near the water. I had been singing and sitting while she had been bothered, or caught. I didn't stop for the burrs as I ran towards her.

Getting closer, I could see that the second figure was a man. Where had he come from so quickly, and what was he doing so close to Hetty, who was sitting up now, facing him? I felt like crying as I ran, and my chest hurt despite the short distance.

They turned towards me as I neared them. Hetty's face was pink, and she was almost smiling in a small way, as though she didn't know what else to do with her face. The man had picked himself up from where he had been kneeling, close to her—and now that I could see the whole of him, I understood that he wasn't really a man. He was an older boy, or perhaps a younger man in his early twenties, and had long hair that was unwashed, and brown arms coming strong out of the sleeves of a red flannie. He didn't look like he was planning to go swimming. There wasn't a smile on his face, this man who had interrupted everything, but he wasn't frowning either, as if I didn't matter enough to him either way.

Hetty wrapped the towel beneath her as far as it would go around her torso, and I watched him reach his hand down towards her thigh and squeeze it until the air was still. Then he turned and began to walk away, and we watched him, and when he was near gone he turned back and said to Hetty in a loud voice, 'Too bad your friend came back, hey?' letting the dust he had kicked walking in his big boots gather around him like a tiny tornado.

After he'd gone, Hetty wouldn't tell me what had happened between them, though I asked her the same question in every way I could think of. She'd never been secretive before, and I couldn't understand the tight face she kept making. I watched her rub at her thigh where his hand had been and hoped she would stop staring out into the distance, until she did, saying sorry, and should we call her mother to come and get us. I remember feeling so separate there next to her, knowing I didn't want or understand whatever it was that she had just had, and that I would one day lose her to this thing I could never give her that she wanted, despite the violence I had smelled in the air when I had seen them together.

After we had gathered our towels and pulled our dry clothes on over our damp bathers, we walked to the house in silence and used Tom's phone to call Hetty's mother, Patricia, who told us to wait on the side of the road for her. We walked to the road and sat on the gravel together, and I wanted to touch Hetty to snap her out of it, but I also didn't want her to sense that I didn't understand.

It was so long before Patricia arrived, the two of us waiting there in silence, but only as the car appeared on the road did

Hetty turn to me. Her face was pale.

'We touched each other a bit. Him first.'

I tried to nod my head, so she would go on. My neck felt like it was broken.

'It wasn't that scary,' she said, and stood up to dust the brown off her dress, the dam coming back through the fabric from her bathers beneath.

MOUTH
the place where the river flows into the sea

As the weeks in Toronto passed, it felt like everyone around me was touching and kissing and lying in bed together. Marjorie was full of new relationships blooming, or old ones reigniting after too many beers at Ronnie's on a Thursday. Steph started inviting over a guy called Morris, who had curled hair and thick arms with meaty hands at their ends. Clark introduced us one morning in the kitchen to his new girlfriend, Isabel, who was so beautiful she was almost annoying. One night after there had been people and drink in the courtyard, I walked into the bathroom to find Steph and Clark entangled. They both told me later that they weren't getting back together, that they were with Morris and Isabel now, and it had only been the alcohol. I'd never even known about the together part, and felt I had no right to an opinion.

Minnie even had someone who started coming to visit on her lunch break, which she had started taking. His name was Paul, and he was very tall and awkward, and made her cheeks turn the colour of a Roncesvalles Avenue sunset.

I stayed me, barely touching my own vagina, not admitting what really made it swell, what caused that flicker in my pelvis to thrash. Not letting myself have a crush on anyone, for fear of who the anyone might turn out to be; watching everyone around me dive deep.

The few boys and then girls I had in my bed through the years before we went to Canada had Hetty's lips and Hetty's lines and arches in the dark, and I let them. I suppose I was in love with her, but I tried to pretend it didn't matter, and I succeeded, mostly. She didn't know, because I knew she didn't feel the same way and I was scared she would try to, so I hid it and encouraged myself to deny it, like a sickly feeling in your gut that you try to pretend isn't the beginning of food poisoning.

Hetty's boyfriend Sean had known. He used to watch me when I would watch her, the furtive pauses I would let myself take, and I heard him yelling at Hetty once that I had a thing for her, and it was so fucking obvious that she was an idiot not to see it. Hetty had told him to shut up, and then they had closed her bedroom door and I could only hear muffled voices, followed by muffled sobs, followed later by muffled moans. I hated that he could see something about me that I had tried to keep hidden. It was like he had come across me naked, and had laughed at the ripe vulnerability of me without my clothes.

I didn't want to have a relationship with anyone, and I definitely didn't want one with Hetty, because I knew it would be a disaster and my heart would end up even more cloistered than it already was. I decided, on the nights when I let myself think about it, that I would be that woman who didn't need anyone. It seemed like I might be able to pull it off, that I could base myself on an old friend of my mum's, who had called herself Juniper, and worn colourful smocks and amethyst stones to take the focus off her loneliness. It wasn't true, anyway, really, that she had been lonely. Juniper seemed one of the most content people I knew—even her walk was more purposeful, her gait more free, than those in relationships around her. Couples were weird: that had always been very obvious to me. The happier they were, the more weird, the more room they took up with all their private specialness, alienating themselves and everyone around them.

~

A few weeks after Hetty had visited Cafe Art Song with Elaine, I made myself cross the road after my shift and walk through the heavy doors of the art gallery for my first visit. No one looked at me when I got inside, in my black jeans and sweatshirt. I smelt a little like bread or milk or sugar, and cheese, like something dense like pasta, but it didn't seem busy in there, and I felt safe in the sound of not many people. I walked around and up the sinuous walkway that led to the ticketing desk and breathed long breaths as I felt the design of the building lean on me. It was beautiful inside as well as out, like the National Gallery in Melbourne with its streaming water wall that made you feel like you were wet from swimming or a water fight when you looked at it, and the grey fort body of the gallery that stood behind.

The woman at the ticket counter told me I could wander

the exhibitions that dotted the building as I wished. It felt kind, the way she pressed the ticket into my hand, encouraging me gently. I left my bag in the cloakroom and set out under the wooden walkway ceiling that Frank Gehry had imagined, up the stairs to the second level. It felt special up there, and because there were not many other people I felt as though I was in a film or a song, almost putting my hands out and closing my eyes to spin my body around and around.

There was a photography exhibition in the main gallery, with its high walls and silent attendants standing in the corners of each room. I imagined they would have soaked in so much excess and metaphor and keenness and energy through their skin, being around art all day, every day. I wondered if it started to get boring. There were beautiful photos all around me, and I decided I would choose a favourite. Usually I did this with Hetty in galleries, and we often chose the same piece. I was determined that day to do it all without her.

It was the photo I stood in front of the longest that I chose—a snapshot of a group of friends having a picnic on some grass next to dark-blue rippled water. They were eating cake, the group of friends, and laughing at something. Some mouths were open; some were pinched into wry smiles. Each wore an outfit I imagined was their favourite, and there were no cleavages, just flat muscled chests half covered by a dress or a pointed collar. I wanted to be part of a group like that. The water behind them was almost aqueous and they would have jumped in after finishing their cake, after the photo was taken. It was a glorious picture, *Picnic on the Esplanade, Boston*—the first time I saw a Nan Goldin.

As I came back out of the photo I noticed the weight of someone near me. I turned and saw standing behind me and to the left a small woman, about my age, with long, wispy brown hair. She smiled when I turned, and moved slightly away, perhaps shy. I turned back and felt myself blush. The woman was pale and possibly plain, she seemed to be nothing, but I could feel the skin of my face and neck was pink from locking eyes with her.

She shuffled behind me, and I heard her footsteps as she walked away from me, on to the next photograph, then the one after that. I didn't want to turn but I did need to know that she was leaving. I couldn't enjoy the art with someone unfamiliar on my skin.

When I finally pulled away from the picnic and looked to where the woman had been, she was gone, and there was only the attendant standing near the door looking at the wall with his hands behind his back. I hoped I wouldn't see her again. I wanted to be the kind of person who went to look at art on their own and didn't need or want to meet anyone, and I really felt like this was who I was that day. Talking to someone interesting and trying to find the right words—linking what I was saying to what was going on inside—seemed so far away from what I was trying to do.

I kept standing long before each photograph, beginning to grasp that every photographer was American, and that I loved most the images of friends or lovers where their eyes were on each other and the camera was an afterthought, or not a thought at all. I decided to get my camera out and use it at Marjorie next time everyone was home and we were all sitting in the courtyard or the living room.

The other part of the gallery I wanted to see was on the lower level. I walked slowly along the balcony that squared an open area full of light, and stepped down the first staircase I saw. The Thomson Collection was on permanent exhibit, and I knew it included a few Emily Carr paintings. I had loved Emily Carr since I started wanting to visit Canada, for her paintings made of wild strokes and brave, thick colours. She painted trees and sky and clouds and grass like a vivid dream made real, and I wanted to see a canvas she had touched. The photo I had seen of Carr in her later years—a large stern woman with thick eyebrows like mine, arms crossed before her—was wonderful to me. She wasn't elegant, or apologetic. She was whole and fierce and unusual, and she saw things in a way that she believed mattered. I could see that in her paintings.

When I'd first discovered Emily Carr's paintings and learned as much as I could about her life, I told Hetty about her. Hetty was a good listener and could become enthusiastic about things that weren't hers. She appreciated every painting I showed her, and loved that Carr had been an explorer, that she had travelled all over the world and stretched herself across Canada so that she could get the most authentic understanding of indigenous Canadian life for her art.

Hetty's favourite Emily Carr painting was *Stumps and Sky*, because she said it could be anywhere, the scene of that painting, that it could be Australia, even though Carr had never been there. *Stumps and Sky* hung at the Art Gallery of Ontario and we had planned to come and see it together, but Hetty seemed to have forgotten, and I didn't want to have to ask—so

I would see it on my own and keep the experience for myself.

I walked through the smaller rooms, muted with their bone-hued walls, watching out for it. There were many beautiful paintings, but I didn't want to stop at any of them in that moment. Finally, around the corner of what was possibly the last doorway, there she was. I walked over and stood just in front, glad to be the only one there.

The painting was oily; and the colours—blue, orange, forest—were brighter than they had been on the internet; and the whooshing of the clouds, their curls and flurries, was moving. I remembered hearing that Carr used expensive, good-quality paint—she came from a family with money and must have thought it senseless not to use some of it for this purpose. Quality paint can last forever, and *Stumps and Sky* looked like it could have been painted a week ago.

The thing I had loved most about the painting, when I first saw it, was the rust-orange colour of the dirt at the bottom of the scene, and—standing in front of the real thing—it was still the best thing about it. I wondered again whether there were parts of Canada that had the same red dirt Australia had, though I was sure this wasn't true, couldn't be true, that I didn't even really want it to be.

As I stood there, rolling my eyes over the up and down of the trees and the horizon, I heard the noise of someone behind me. I turned and saw that it was the girl with the long brown hair. She was standing looking at a painting on the opposite wall, of a man standing in the snow in a wooden coat with a dog next to him, and I took the time to see what she was wearing and leave my eyes on her a little longer. She had blue jeans on, and a red-and-white-striped top, and stood compact, sure, like a dancer.

I took a breath and let it out, then another. I made sure they were quiet, those breaths. I turned back towards *Stumps and Sky* and wondered if she was as thoughtful as she seemed to be, standing there. I wondered whether she was wondering anything about me, whether she had even realised I was the same person as the person she had seen before, up there in the wooden sky.

'Hi,' I heard from behind me. A small, round voice, like a circle.

I turned and saw her smiling. She wasn't plain at all, really. Rather she was pretty in a noiseless way.

'Oh, hi,' I answered, trying to stay as still as possible so I didn't go red or wobble my words in my throat. There wasn't enough time to think about what to say before I needed to say something else. 'Do you like Emily Carr?'

I hoped I didn't sound like I was trying to prove that I knew the name of an artist, but she smiled, revealing fingerprint dimples in both cheeks. Then she laughed. 'I don't know who Emily Carr is! Is that bad?'

'Oh no! No! She's the only artist I've ever known the name of, ever. It's just that this is a painting of hers'—I pointed at *Stumps and Sky*, its vivid blue and red—'and I came here to see it.'

She smiled again. She didn't seem to feel the need to say as much as me.

'But no!' I repeated, and then stopped, telling myself not to say anything else, even if the silence became unbearable, even if the air split in two.

'Oh good,' she said, making those dimples deeper. Her little hands were by her sides, and I let myself look at her eyes. They were brown and curved, like kidney beans.

She walked to stand next to me and I turned back around and we both looked at the Emily Carr. This time I saw how carefully Carr had made the wind and the clouds look like the essence of wind and clouds and not just swirls of white paint, and how there must have been the beginning or middle or ending of a storm on the day or night that she painted the scene.

'It's beautiful.' She said it with certainty, and I nodded.

'It is.'

She told me her name was Faith, and I told her that my name was Ness. We stood in front of the Emily Carr and she told me she hated her name—her parents were born-again Christians and had her later than most people had children, after finding themselves able to under the protective shadow of God. They had named her in honour of it all, and she thought that was concerning, as if she embodied something that wasn't real. I noticed that she had the lightest of dark circles under each of her kidney-bean eyes.

She looked at me squarely, carefully. 'Are you Australian?'

It was the first time since I'd arrived in Canada that someone had picked it.

'Yes,' I said, and tried not to beam.

'What's it like there?' she asked.

'It's big, so it's different all over. I'm from Melbourne, which I guess is kind of like here a bit, and it's cold sometimes there, but gets very hot too. We have lots of bushfires.'

'I didn't know it got cold in Australia. I don't know much about it, actually. Which is terrible.'

'That's not terrible. There's not much to know about Australia. It's big and there aren't many people living there. Just a big selfish island!'

She laughed bigger this time and I heard a slight shriek at the end. I liked it when people had strange laughs. It was like a small bit of eccentricity that they usually hid was revealed every time they found something funny.

'You know that we're perpetually drunk there, yeah?'

She laughed and let out that small shriek again. 'Yes, I had heard that. So it's true, eh?'

'I'm drunk right now!'

Her laugh made me want to kiss her, suddenly and overwhelmingly. She opened her mouth and closed her eyes and leaned her head back, and I saw the pale of her neck, just briefly. There seemed to be a smile she would make only after she laughed like that. It was a smile like she had more to let out but was too shy to. Her mouth held together tight and creased to stop it.

I'd never walked through a gallery with someone like her. We looked at every painting in the Thomson Collection and said things to each other about each one. When I looked at art with Hetty she would always ask me to tell her what it was about. I would leave feeling exhausted, questioning every answer I had given, all of my understanding. Faith seemed to have ideas about what each artist had been trying to do, but she didn't sit within those thoughts like they were important. I felt myself spreading out around us, covering every piece with my eyes and my sticky fingers and the saliva trails of my tongue.

When we finished and the gallery was closing and we seemed to be the last ones there except for the attendants still at their corners, drooping slightly, we walked together through the heavy glass and wood doors, and stood awkwardly opposite each other at angles on the concrete outside. I could smell heat and light, and Faith had a sheen on her skin, and we smiled at each other with the corners of our mouths and our eyes.

'It was so nice to meet you,' I said, my heart banging against my ribs.

'Oh, you too!' she replied, her mouth curling slightly at one side.

We agreed to meet again, this time face to face, sitting down across the table from one another. Faith said goodbye, and I said goodbye, and I pulled myself away from her and walked down the steps to Beverley Street. I felt my heels kicking up slightly as I walked past Grange Park and down towards Shoppers Drugmart. She was already making me move differently. I was green and lush inside.

RIA
the sinking of a river valley

A party at Marjorie was planned for the birthdays of Dill, Clark and Ingrid, all within the first week of summer. It was getting so hot in the middle of the day that it felt damp inside the kitchen at Cafe Art Song and I could smell wilting daylilies as I walked home each evening. I decided to invite Faith along, to see her among others, to put some pressure on this thing I hoped I was feeling. I wondered whether she found parties as difficult as I did. Maybe it would be different here, anyway. Back in Melbourne the parties had been full of people from school I had never known how to talk to, and too many old memories for the possibility of new ones.

    I got home from work in the late afternoon and was met at the door by Steph, who told me she was off to get the alcohol. I asked her to buy me three long bottles of beer and pressed money into her hot hand twice before she would accept it. She asked me if I had invited anyone but I didn't feel like telling her—not because I wanted to keep anything secret, and not because I was ashamed that I felt things for Faith, but because I just didn't feel like spreading myself out and waiting for reactions. She would meet Faith if Faith came, and she would draw her own conclusions, wonder her own wonders, or think nothing of it at all.

Steph was so kind and tried to be unassuming, I could tell, but she could see things and maybe even read my mind if I let myself think about it for too long, because she had green eyes that grew up your neck and became a flower on your face before you could stop them near your chin. She smiled, and rubbed my shoulder before she jumped down the steps, and I knew she would likely know what Faith might be to me as soon as she met her.

It was hot in our bedroom and Hetty wasn't there so I took off my jeans and my shirt and lay on top of the doona in my bra and undies, watching my tummy lift up and down slightly as I breathed in the thick air and let it slowly back out. The undies were old and tight, and cut across my belly. I hadn't noticed all day at work, wearing them under my jeans as I crossed from kitchen to floor, or on the walk home, but now the feeling was unbearable. I reached down and pulled them off—down my legs and over my toes—and threw them at my corner of the room. I could smell myself, and I liked the smell. It was rich and hungry, and made me remember I was full of lots of things. I thought about the party and felt tiny flutters in my stomach. I was always nervous in my stomach before a party.

I wondered where Hetty was. There wasn't much of her in the room, really, if I looked around from where I lay. She didn't own much, hadn't brought much with her from Melbourne and had accrued nothing since being here that I could see. Most of what she had here was still in her pack in the corner, a favourite spot of Whitney's to curl up on top of and sleep. I guessed she had some things at work with her, or she kept them in the multicoloured bag she always had slung against her hip. The room was mostly Whitney's and a little bit mine. Hetty was hardly anywhere, and I missed her.

It was still warm when people started knocking on the front door of Marjorie, their arms full of drink, an energy in their eyes and bodies and voices. I had changed into a long skirt and blouse, the only special things I owned, and could feel my thighs rubbing against each other underneath. It wasn't uncomfortable, but it did remind me of my body as I walked from lounge to kitchen to yard. I wondered when Faith would arrive. I took gulps of the fat bottle of Molson that Steph had bought me and felt the slow bubbles pop in my head.

I watched Dill and Clark and Ingrid talk and laugh with their smudged pink lips and tongues, from the big bowl of raspberry punch Steph had mixed, complete with floating cherries and edible flowers that looked like yellow butterflies resting on its surface. I stood in the kitchen and spoke to Clark and Isabel and their friend Lou about the Australian summer—how even in Melbourne there would be stretches where it would be over forty degrees for days on end—and they told me they wanted to go there, like everyone did, and that they loved Australia already. I listened to Dill talk to a tiny girl with gold shoulders and tried to work out if he was waiting for Hetty. My Molson bottle emptied and I opened another one.

After I had been offered some of the punch and a glass of Ingrid's wine and my eyes were warm in their sockets, Hetty arrived with Elaine. They piled into the living room in the middle of a private joke, and Hetty looked at me with eyes that told me she was drunk already, that she wasn't really there. My body tightened with Elaine near me—I could feel it in my shoulders and my lifted clavicle. I watched as Hetty fell against her and giggled, and Elaine lifted Hetty's chin head and said, 'You're such a bitch!' It wasn't funny to me, this crude show, and I was disappointed.

The drinks made my thoughts fluorescent. Despite disliking Elaine and feeling she was not the right kind of friend for Hetty, I knew why they were spending time together. Hetty craved defiance, and I couldn't give it to her. I sometimes wished I was the kind of person who would tell a friend what was useful, that I wasn't so often afraid of the potential for hurt feelings and a fight that I would be the cause of; but I wasn't and I couldn't be, and I had to come to some sort of peace with that. I would always have to share Hetty with these friends she would make throughout life who rubbed up against her and pulled her up and down. I couldn't change it.

I decided I would go and stand in the courtyard with Ingrid's friends, who were dancing and sharing cigarettes and tying the fairy lights around their foreheads, but Hetty was saying something to me, loud and near now.

'Can I talk to you?' she asked, her face close with hot breath. I nodded.

'We can go up to our bedroom,' she said, as if that was something special. It was tiring: the pull of her booze eyes and the pull at my arm with her skinny fingers that didn't know what they were doing. I wished she hadn't come home.

We saw Whitney on the stairs on the way up, cowering against the wall with her plush hair standing, her eyes angry at the noise and the house full of people she didn't know. Hetty bent down to pat her and slipped, letting me grab at her sides before she fell. Once we were in our room, she closed the door and flopped on the bed, letting the air out of her mouth loudly.

I wanted her to know I wasn't just full of time for her. She had been with Elaine and now she was a wreck. I couldn't clean that up.

'What is it, Hetty?'

She lifted herself up off the doona slowly, looked at me and sighed. 'I think Elaine likes me.'

I sighed. Of course she did. Everyone did. I did. Dill likely did. The whole party downstairs probably dreamed of having Hetty next to them; of kissing her neck, of hearing her and knowing her sounds were theirs.

'Yeah. She probably does. Do you like her?'

At this, Hetty groaned, and scratched her arms. I noticed that some of her nails were bloody around the edges.

'No. Not like that. She's tough. And she's funny. But I don't like girls in that way—not really. And she looks at me so intensely sometimes. I don't understand it.'

She didn't even look up at me as she said this, and I reminded myself once again that she hadn't guessed how I felt, how I sometimes let myself feel, about her. It almost made me angry, how she was just out there in the world, being gentle and gorgeous and callow, never stopping to wonder what that might do to people.

Hetty sat up again then, and patted the bed next to her. I walked over and sat down.

'The thing is,' she said in a low voice, looking at me sideways, 'sometimes she says things I can't quite hear, under her breath, and it scares me.'

The air around us stopped.

'What do you mean?' I asked.

'I know it sounds weird, but that's what I mean. She says things under her breath. I ask her to repeat them but she denies even saying anything at all.'

'Okay…But what do you think she's saying?'

'I don't know! It's weird. She says I'm imagining it. But I'm not. It's like tiny whispers.'

Hetty was picking at her nails. I could see dabs of red on the pads of her fingers where the blood had moved. She sighed heavily, as if she needed to hold each breath in as long as she possibly could before she let it out.

'And she used to cut herself. All up her arms and down her legs. With a Stanley knife. Not anymore, but it's so sad, Ness. I don't know how to make sure she's okay.'

I remembered those white lines trailing the inside of Elaine's arms: the only vulnerable thing about her on that day out the front of Cafe Art Song. Knowing she had cut those lines herself was knowing she understood pain.

'But, Hetty, I don't know what you're trying to say. Is she being a bitch? Then stop being friends with her. If she makes you feel uncomfortable and then denies it, you need to do something.'

It seemed to me that Elaine wasn't the type of person who would say anything under her breath. I couldn't quite picture it—yet Hetty was so upset.

'I don't know! I don't know. I don't think she's being a bitch but it's just weird. I feel weird.'

I took her hands in mine and turned the fingers over. 'Stop hurting yourself. Please.'

She laughed, lightly, and pulled one of her hands away to pat me.

~

Faith didn't come to the party. I didn't text to ask her why, but I waited in my skirt and my lace-collared shirt until one in the morning and didn't see her come towards me, smiling, as I had imagined. My body felt tired, and the hope I'd been holding quietly in my tummy left, leaving nothing but fizz.

That night I went to bed hours before Hetty but was awake when she crept in, the shadow of her body in the street light hunched over, as if that might help her keep quiet. She lay down next to me, smelling of meat and cigarettes. When I finally fell asleep the dreams were chaos.

COVE
the smallest indentation

Halfway through summer I started to know Toronto's streets and to feel like I was supposed to be walking along them, up them, down them. There was a warm drench to the city's air in July, and I tried to enjoy the way my body moved through it. The doors of Marjorie, front and back and side, were left open to greet the breeze, and Whitney cooled herself under the leaves of our backyard oak, her fluffy tummy splayed against the bricks.

    After Faith had missed the party, she'd texted me to say she was sorry, and we met for a beer at Cold Tea, deep in the compost of Kensington Market. Across the bench from one another in the damp courtyard, we shared things and looked at each other shyly and then once we were drunk in a brazen way that made my throat open, we kissed in the dirty white corridor outside where an old man sat peeling carrots on a milk crate, and walked hand in hand across the pedestrian streets until she left me at my door.

Faith was from London, a town in Ontario two hours to the south. She had known she liked girls since she was five, and had kissed her best friend when they were eight and pretending to get married. Faith was the groom, and said she realised then that she never wanted to be the bride or the groom but that she had really liked kissing her friend. When she suggested they do it again a week later the girl said no, and never spoke to Faith again. She circled girls after that, watching the ones she liked carefully, to see if they might be like her. In late high school she slept with a close friend who said she was 'confused' and later broke Faith's heart. She had her first relationship at uni, with the young tutor of her Studies in Poetics subject, who was awkward and passionate and devoted, and she had been with a few other women since.

Faith had told her parents, and rolled her eyes when she told me her mother had asked her, 'Oh, but are you sure?' and had later tried to make up for this with a celebration dinner. She didn't share much about her father: his reaction or his presence in her life. He seemed to be inconsequential rather than devastating in his silence, and I thought I possibly understood. I told Faith I envied her the celebration roast chicken and lemon-meringue pie, and that I hadn't told my parents because there didn't seem much point.

After we saw each other that night and confirmed the curiosity that flitted around us like street-lamp moths, we texted each other small parts of ourselves, like offerings. Faith told me that the only thing in the whole world that she truly enjoyed doing was reading. That when people spoke about the importance of doing what you were passionate about, doing what you lost yourself in, she always wondered what job there was that required only curling up on the couch with a good book. She seemed to think this meant she was fundamentally boring, but it was appealing to me. She lost herself easily in the stories of others. I wished I could do that.

She told me in one of her long, winding texts that her favourite author, Margaret Atwood, lived in Toronto, and that she had this hope sitting like a jewel in her belly that one day she would see her. I had read one of Atwood's novels, *The Robber Bride*, and found it dense and dangerous. Faith told me she had too, and that Atwood's books were almost always like that—raw and dark and full, and full of pain, like sacrifices. I googled Margaret Atwood to see what she looked like and found a small, bright-faced woman with sprigs of white curl around her head. Faith told me that Atwood shopped at a Korean supermarket near where Faith lived, on Bloor Street West in Korea Town, and that she had spent far too many hours there quietly browsing and waiting, but had never seen her.

I stopped myself from suggesting we stake out the place together. I was trying not to do all the things I wanted to do—ask Faith to stay over, kiss her stomach and touch her hair, tell her I already knew that I would fall in love with her. A wrong part of me wanted to tell her that she had taken over the space that was usually filled with Hetty, as if that would prove how excited I was, but I made sure I didn't talk about Hetty much with her. Faith sensed things. She would know, if she heard enough, how complicated my feelings had been for so long.

I told Hetty about Faith one night in bed with the moon

shining in on us. It was past midnight but I couldn't sleep, and when Hetty crept in I told her I was awake.

'I met a girl at the gallery,' I said, my head propped up with my elbow, not able to hide my smile.

'Ness! How exciting! What's her name?'

It was funny that Hetty and I had never really talked about how I was gay. I had modelled this by never bringing it up, after I stopped going out with boys and started trying things with girls because I had to or I would have burst, and Hetty had simply followed me into the cave. Sometimes it made me angry, as if her silence was confirmation of how ashamed I should be; but I knew this wasn't true. Hetty just didn't think it was a big deal, and didn't think we needed to talk about it unless I wanted to. She was so gentle sometimes it felt like laziness, or something more sinister like self-absorption. Her reaction that night reminded me that she was really only full of love.

'Faith. She hates it.'

Hetty laughed. 'Why? Faith's a beautiful name!'

'Because her parents are crazy.'

I told her how keen I was on Faith and how scary it was to be so keen so quickly, and how I was so worried I would ruin it with my knotted hair or my face or my personality. I told her about our kiss next to the old man peeling carrots, and how I hadn't even felt embarrassed, but that now I was embarrassed, because I was so full and open, and it was exhausting.

'Have you seen her since then, or just texted?' Hetty asked.

'Just texted. I don't want to suggest something else in case she gets scared.'

Hetty was sitting up now, and holding her teddy from childhood, Bear, in her arms.

'When you were with her it wasn't scary, it didn't sound like it was, but now you're away from her maybe you're forgetting that.'

I had hoped Faith would be the one to suggest we see each other again, but it didn't really matter. She seemed to have a full life. If I wanted to be a part of that I might need to make sure of it myself.

'Yes, that's true.'

'You like her; it feels good. Go with it.'

'But she's so *good*. She's just so good and perfect and pretty, and when I think about her I feel like I'm going to vomit.'

'That's beautiful, Nessy,' Hetty murmured, then laughed. She was an angel, lying there, listening to me, but I didn't feel the pull I usually did, to touch her or lie down beside her very close.

I sent Faith a text asking if she wanted to have dinner, Hetty clapping her hands next to me on the bed and telling me I was brave, and then we talked about how our weeks had been since the party, and I asked about Elaine and whether she was still acting in the strange way Hetty had described. The question seemed to change her and she sat up in the bed, her eyes glinting.

'Yes, she's still doing it,' she said, then whispered, 'but she thinks I don't realise.'

'Have you spoken to her about it again?'

'There's no point. She pretends I'm crazy. Yesterday she yelled at me about it.'

I loathed Elaine. She didn't deserve Hetty's sweetness, her deluded loyalty. I wondered why Hetty was so reckless with her own emotional safety, where she had learned to devalue herself. It must have been her father, I decided: how difficult he found it to care about himself, his need always for something more.

Hetty's body had dropped and she was looking at the cover of the doona, which she held in her hand, rubbing it between her fingers and whimpering a little.

'What happened?'

'She says I'm putting my own anxiety onto her and that she can't do anything to help me unless I admit it.' Hetty was crying now, quiet tears drowning her cheeks. 'I don't know what to do.'

'You need to let her go, Hetty. She's nasty.'

'But what if she's right?'

'Her saying things under her breath isn't your fault! It's weird, and she's manipulating you because she's cruel.'

Hetty started to sob then, her thin body shaking with the effort of it, and I put my hand on her shoulder to steady her. I'd never seen her so fragile—Elaine had swallowed her whole.

I got us some glasses of bourbon from a bottle someone had left downstairs at the party, and gave her one to wet her lips with. She was murmuring, and after we drank she lay and slept quickly. It was nice to have her there next to me while I sat and looked at a book, not reading the words, waiting for Faith to reply. If I could have made her stay there forever I would have. She huffed little snores and occasionally moved herself over and around and back and forth, as if it was hard to stay still for the dreams.

Faith replied suggesting we meet for rice and beans and kingfish on Queen Street the next day, followed by ice-cream sandwiches. My stomach jumped about. I hoped she wouldn't realise I was boring.

I lay down in the moonlit, street-lit room and thought about Elaine and Hetty. In the same way that Hetty helped me smile, the way her personality and how she talked and moved made me feel pleasant and calm, Elaine moved me to lurch, to feel a tightening in my chest that I didn't fully understand but that was hard not to react to. I didn't often hate people, and it usually took a lot more rudeness than I'd had from Elaine before I became impatient. I would have been glad never to see her again, and could feel myself becoming more protective of Hetty. I wanted to drag her body away from Elaine's—to show her what I could see from where I was standing.

I remembered, lying there, the book my mum had often had on her bedside table when I was growing up. She'd told me one afternoon to have a read of it, after I'd sat on the frill of her doona and told her I was having problems with a girl at school who I believed was too bossy, too confident of her own power, more popular than I thought she deserved to be. Mum had listened—she was a good listener when she was well enough, nodding often with her soft head—and then she had asked whether I thought it could be possible that there was a part of me that wanted to be confident, to be brash, to not always worry what others were thinking inside their heads, the way this girl was. I didn't think I did, and I said so. Mum picked up the book and handed it to me. She told me to read it, and shook herself down under the covers again for a bit more sleep.

The book was called *The Dark Side of the Light Chasers*. It told me that everyone has a shadow, and that we can hide our shadows so well, bury them so deep, that when we meet someone who has embraced theirs we might become defensive, hostile. I imagined now what it would be like to drop my layers and be like Elaine—direct, unsentimental. Maybe my shadow was sick of hiding, and recognised in her something true. I fell asleep before I could decide on a way to find out.

WELL
an issue of water from the earth

I grew very fond of my Marjorie housemates.

Ingrid was easy to be around and so open about how she was feeling at any moment, on any day. She was pretty and petite and kind, and sometimes had her best friend Jill with her, who was tall and solid. They included me easily in their conversations, and asked me questions as if they cared about me. Ingrid was Whitney's real owner and loved her with a silly ferocity. She was the reason Whitney's belly hung low and round when she walked, from too many fish biscuits.

Robin was always getting up very late or very early and wearing beautiful outfits he had made himself out of shiny paper or mosquito netting. His irreverence was the kind that could become sincerity very quickly, and he seemed to really like me; he would touch me on the arm often, and look into my eyes to see how I was really feeling. Robin and Clark were close, and I wondered if Robin loved Clark the way I loved Hetty.

Clark was straight, and attractive in his asymmetry and the way his body moved like a flag on a boat in a windy sea. He was tall and his limbs were long, and he had crooked teeth and big, bouncy hair. His laugh was like the call of a walrus and he didn't seem to take anything seriously. I didn't often see Clark alone—he worked late into the night as a pharmacist at a twenty-four-hour clinic on University Avenue and had a lot of friends. He was nice to be around because he made fun of himself: it reminded me of Australia. He was less conscientious than the others, and more brash and nonchalant. I relaxed in his company.

The relationship that Clark had been in with Steph before they both lived at Marjorie had been a long one. I couldn't imagine them together, despite Ingrid and Robin and Steph herself telling me they were inseparable for four years. Steph was calm and contained, her body athletic and her face quietly handsome. She had toast-coloured skin and blond hair, and paused throughout conversations in order to hear and understand. I liked her immensely, but often felt shy when I was with her—large in my movements, loud in my voice. Of all of them, I wished I knew Steph best. She seemed to have so much to her that I felt sad I might never know.

Dill was home more than the others. He worked part-time standing behind the counter at BMV Books, the cheapest bookshop in the city, and was trying to write a novel the rest of the time. He spent long hours at the kitchen table, tousled, sipping at drinks he seemed to take longer than necessary to prepare. He was a joy to come upon, would joke about the cliche he felt he was and slurp at his mug and make me laugh even when I had hoped no one would be home, or out of bed, so I could slink back upstairs and keep to myself.

He was writing something about how it was to be an uncommon type of boy, then an uncommon type of young man; how it was hard to go against the way men were expected to be, and how other men could push this and make it worse. He told me he didn't really expect the book ever to come to anything, but he wanted to write it so his dad could read it one day, and the men he went to school with, and maybe some of his male teachers. He said they hadn't understood him because he wasn't quite the same, and it had taken him until now to know that that was their fault, not his.

I was almost in love with Dill in that way that means you think someone is wonderful but know you would never actually need to hold them. His face was dear, with a large mouth and white teeth and cheeks that stretched when he laughed, and he listened and spoke; just enough of each. Sometimes we would talk to Whitney, who liked to be near us and would curl up against one of the legs of the kitchen table or in one of our laps. Dill would ask her questions in his regular voice and answer them in her little voice, then would ask me questions in her little voice so that I had to answer: sweet, silly questions like, 'What is the thing you most love about my fur?' When he got up to pour more hot water into his cup, or to make toast with butter and banana and honey, I would watch his body when he wasn't facing me. He moved beautifully, and was both small and broad-shouldered.

~

Early one afternoon when we were the only ones home and Dill had asked me to sit with him because he had run out of ways to try to write, I told him about Faith. She was always at the front of my mind, and Dill indulged me, asking me question after question about what she was like and how I felt about what she was like, and smiling big and creased at my answers. He didn't seem to know or not know that I liked girls, just knew and didn't know and was okay with whatever it was that I was. I told him Faith was very beautiful, and that he would think so too. He told me that of course she was.

'I thought maybe you loved Hetty,' he said, after I had finished.

I was embarrassed. My feelings for Hetty must have been so obvious. I thought I hid it well, by moving my eyes the right way and looking at the right things at the right time, catching glimpses of Hetty and smiling only sometimes when she said something gorgeous. It was hard to learn that I wasn't controlling what I put out into the world.

Dill rubbed my hand where it lay limp on the wooden table.

'I shouldn't have said that. I'm sorry.'

I didn't want someone to feel bad because I was unable to keep myself inside my skin. I was spilling out around myself and making people uncomfortable, and to realise it made my face feel hot and red.

'No, Dill, don't be sorry. It's not your fault I'm pathetic!'

I wanted him to know I didn't have illusions that Hetty and I would be together, that she would ever love me in that way. He would understand that it was complicated if I explained, but I didn't feel like doing that. I did want to make sure he didn't feel sorry for me, because that made me feel awkward and soggy and dull, and I knew I didn't need his pity. I was moving further away from Hetty's body every day. It felt like one of us was swimming and the other was nowhere near the water.

'You're not pathetic. At all.'

'It's sort of complicated. I mean, I do love her, but the feeling isn't like what it used to be. And I don't want to be with her or anything—'

'I get it,' he said, and gave me a bright grin. 'She's a babe. But she's crazy too, right?'

I had wondered if others had been noticing Hetty's skittishness. She was moving closer to some imaginary light since she'd met Elaine, and the drugs weren't helping. I didn't know what she was taking or how much, but some nights her bright round pupils and the crashing of her teeth against each other worried me.

'She's been funny lately,' I said.

'Yeah. I've noticed that. It's like she's always on her way somewhere but she's not really sure where she's going.'

'I know. I'm worried about her.'

We talked about Hetty for hours that day. Dill told me he had a big crush on her, and that she had seemed to have one on him too, but over the past few weeks he hadn't been able to crack her face or feel like he was really speaking to her. She would flit in at night and sleep all day. He'd hoped they might kiss, and talk more, and he was sad that they hadn't—he'd wondered whether she was just trying to tell him without telling him that there was no chance.

I told him that it was more than him and her, and that I would talk to her about our worry. Then I felt anxious for the rest of the day, like we had spoken about something that hadn't really been true but now was.

That night it was just me and Dill and Robin at home, and we sat in the living room with bowls of a dark curry that Robin had made, full of vegetables I almost recognised. He cooked well, Robin—cooked often for us, never fazed by extra mouths. He seemed to be able to make something good out of anything we had in the fridge. I'd often watch him in the kitchen, chopping and scraping and inspecting, and finally stirring and tasting. His instinct for texture and heat reminded me of a cat.

Whitney would sit near him on the kitchen floor as he danced the floor back and forth with pinches of salt and wooden spoons. Occasionally she would stand and make her way towards his legs, if they were still, and she would rub against them ferociously. Robin's legs were thin, like the rest of him, and he would laugh at how close she got to toppling him over.

That night we talked about Robin's new boyfriend. Robin told us that when he was with Josh, he often wondered if he even liked him, but he would let Josh kiss him and plan their next date together, and introduce Robin to all his friends. Robin said he often did this—chose men who were not quite what he wanted, so he would not need to be so scared and sad if one day they were gone. I understood this.

Dill asked questions. He had a different way of being in the world from Robin and me. He was confident, hoping and trying for what he really wanted, and wasn't disordered in the way he thought about himself or what he deserved.

Robin tried to explain to Dill how it felt to be constantly wary of affection because it felt too good to last, and then I tried to explain it, and Dill seemed to understand as much as he could by the time we had finished and there was no more curry and Robin presented us with a bottle of wine from the fridge. I remember the way Dill tried to say there was no reason for us to doubt that we were loveable, and that we both laughed.

Then Hetty walked in. She was a little wobbly as she moved towards the table, but after she sat down she seemed to still. I reminded myself to ask her directly what she was using, when we were alone. I hadn't wanted to force it out of her, but it wasn't possible to keep pretending nothing was going on when every time she came home she flopped around like a caught fish.

Hetty eyed us all, with our glasses of pink drink, and told us she was tired. There was no nod towards me, no hint that she cared. I was extra-sensitive around her these days, waiting for signs and clues and declarations that would prove the strength of our friendship, but she wasn't giving me anything.

Robin asked her questions, slowly, and Dill and I watched. Hetty crossed one leg over the other and then swapped them, running her fingers through her flattened hair.

'I'm so tired,' she said, after Robin had asked her how her work at the bar was going.

'I'm sorry,' she said, looking at me. 'I'm always complaining.'

'No, you're not,' I said, trying to hold her eyes with mine. 'You're not.'

'It feels like I am.'

Hetty said this as if it should be light, but there wasn't quite the energy needed in her voice. She rolled back her shoulders one by one, their peaks just skin over curved bone. I kept hearing what sounded like small sighs, but her mouth was closed, her eyes lazy.

I looked at Dill. He was looking at Hetty with something sad around his mouth, and his eyes. She hadn't acknowledged him once that I had noticed, and I could imagine his heart would be hurting. She was almost being unkind. Dill didn't say anything, didn't ask her any questions. He seemed to have accepted that he wasn't really in the room.

'I got a new tattoo!' Hetty exclaimed, out of nowhere, after Robin had stopped asking questions and I had started rubbing at Whitney's neck to distract myself from the silence.

Instantly I felt hurt that she hadn't asked me to come with her to get it. We would never have done something like that without the other when we lived in Melbourne. Every memory I had that was special had Hetty in it, and now she was making all these memories without me, as though it was necessary or normal. I tried to soothe myself. Things were different now, and that might be okay.

I looked up and saw that she wasn't pulling up her top or rolling up her sleeve or her pulling her skirt back. She was just sitting: still lazily, still a little bit slumped.

'Where? What did you get?'

She shook herself out of something and smiled. 'On the small of my back.'

Hetty stood up, and turned around. She was wearing a long singlet that covered most of her skirt and was made of some-thing like jersey. She pulled up the back of the singlet and exposed her pale pink-white skin. There was no tattoo—just a few small freckles and the surface of her.

'Ha ha.' Robin was standing in the doorway to the kitchen now, and said this in a long, flat voice a little different from his usual one.

'Is it okay? Do you like it?'

Hetty kept standing there with her spindly arms holding up the jersey that had been covering nothing, and I felt a deep sorry feeling and realised that I had never felt sorry for her before. There was no tattoo. Why was she confused?

I wished Robin and Dill would leave. I wished, even though I valued them so much, that they had never been there at all. Hetty's body and mind seemed to need privacy.

She let one of her hands touch the small of her back softly, and said *Ouch* in a tiny voice that made me scared. My heart started to beat so fast I could feel a pulsing in my eyelids. I looked over at Robin, who motioned at Dill to come into the kitchen with him. They closed the door.

'Het, sit down, babe,' I said.

I walked over and gently helped her pull her top back down and get herself onto the couch again. She made a few small noises and leaned over to pat Whitney, who was curled on the carpet below us.

My mouth felt so dry I had to drag my tongue around in it, dispersing what moisture was left. I wanted to know why Hetty was so often out of it these days, and what she had been taking. It felt like I needed to be the kind of friend they have in American movies—kind, strong, sure. A friend who could do an intervention.

'Het, what's been going on lately? You're different.'

She looked up at me from where she had sunk down into the folds. She was shaking her head.

'Nothing, Ness. I'm just drinking too much, I guess. You know how I do that sometimes.'

Her hand came up as if to touch my arm but dropped back down. Everything about her seemed to be fading.

'Have you been eating enough?'

Hetty had always been funny about food. She was the kind of person who didn't think of eating very often, and when she wasn't going well it dropped from her mind completely. She enjoyed the taste of delicious things when she did sit down to eat them, but could go days without doing so. I had often wondered what she did with all that time so many of us spent thinking about, preparing or eating food. She'd laughed and shook her head when I told her I envied her. She had told me many times she wished she loved food too.

'Yes. Elaine makes me a toasted sandwich every night at work.'

'What does she put in it?'

Hetty sighed. 'I don't know, Ness. Baked beans, cheese? One time she put eggs in there for me and they cooked fluffy and hot.'

She moved her head against the couch cushion, like a cat against a leg. Her eyes were closing.

I wondered if I should tell her there was no tattoo on her back. I was worried she would be scared, or wouldn't understand, or would say something that made even less sense.

'What have you been taking, Hetty?'

'What?' She lifted her head up and took in my expression. 'Nothing.'

There was a long silence. I was determined not to fill it.

'I took some mushrooms with Elaine a few times, but that was weeks ago.'

I hadn't known this, but it still didn't explain why Hetty was balancing on the edge of something now, or had fallen in.

'And I had a few wines before I left work. Lately I seem to be getting drunk so quickly...' Her voice trailed off and she closed her eyes again.

I felt like I should be worrying about her losing consciousness, but there was no reason to. She was tired because she was working too much and not eating enough and drinking too often. I couldn't do much about any of that, and I didn't worry that she wasn't telling the truth. It was important to try to let some of her go.

'Okay, Het. Sorry to hound you. Let's go up to bed.'

We walked upstairs together, Hetty groaning with every step, telling me she never exercised anymore, that she was so unfit, that her heart was fatty and broken. We sat on the bed and planned the adventures that we would have together, soon, when we could both take the time. I didn't believe the words, and tried to think about Faith instead as we shifted down into sleep. Her body was hot in my head, and I basked briefly in it.

My mind went back to Hetty on the couch, slumped; Hetty standing with her thin body, showing me something that wasn't there; Hetty so tired she couldn't explain herself, or help me understand. She started to snore quickly, and I tried to hold the noise inside to remind myself that she was fine.

When I slept I had dream after dream of Hetty sleeping, of her covered in tattoos. In one she had a tattooed face, and her lips and her eyebrows didn't move when she talked. She told me she was hungry but she couldn't eat, because her mouth wouldn't open. Then she turned into Elaine, the way people do in dreams—morphing so surreptitiously I didn't question it at all. When Elaine started to laugh at me, I walked away, looking for Hetty throughout a windowless, doorless house. There were baked beans splattered on every wall, slimy like the insides of a body.

MERE
a sheet of water, standing

Faith met me after work one afternoon in late August, when Toronto was hot bricks and turgid afternoons. We had been seeing each other for over a month, in an official sort of way, though neither of us had come out and asked the other if we were girlfriends. I was starting to know what her body felt like when I was holding parts of it, and feeling a little more like myself when I was around her, but it was still scary to see her and be reminded of how much I cared.

It had been a busy morning at Cafe Art Song, with a group of older women coming for cake and coffee and then lunch before a gallery tour. They had been joyful and raucous—howling into their milkshakes and choking on their stews with crusty rolls as one or another told a joke or reminded the others of a silly time in their past. I hoped I would have a group of friends like that when I was older. They seemed free, and sure of themselves. They smiled generously when Minnie and I came to check on them, or delivered their orders, their kindness easy. Minnie and I told each other how much we liked them when we passed in the kitchen, and by the time my shift was ending I felt I should say goodbye and thank them as I left.

Faith was wearing a dress that looked like a neat sack tied at her waist with a long stretch of rope, and her hair was curled into a little bun. She looked pretty and clean, despite the wet and roaring heat. We sat down at one of the tables at the front of the cafe and looked at each other, and Faith asked me about my shift. She seemed to understand the weird feeling like love that I was having for the group of older women who had been our customers for hours, and told me her favourite thing to do was to watch groups of older women. Their proud chaos made her feel optimistic, she said, as if being female got better with age.

Minnie brought out a small bowl of pistachios hiding in their shells and little glasses of lemon soda with floating rosemary sprigs for us, and I introduced her to Faith. They smiled at each other and said they had heard a lot about one another while I broke the shell away from a small green nut and ate it.

'What would you like to do tonight?' Faith asked me, after Minnie had left us.

I hadn't thought about what we might do—a sign I was becoming more at ease with the idea of Faith and me. She was so polite sometimes—too polite to tell me what she wanted, for fear it would make me feel as if I had to want it too. I had noticed that many times in Canada—the conscientious politeness; the dedication to never telling other people quite what they thought or what to do, in case it was too much. I hadn't realised how direct Australians were, how direct I was, in my own way. Sometimes I felt like a brazen weed yellowing at the edge of a manicured lawn.

I suggested we take the streetcar down to The Beaches, in the east of Toronto. I'd not visited this area, but I liked the name and wanted to see if the picture in my head was anything like the reality. Faith told me she hadn't visited there for years, but remembered it had felt like she was on holiday when she had, sauntering along the boardwalk and browsing the many shops selling ice cream and beach towels. To have a part of the city called The Beaches in a place that has lake water at its edge seemed odd, and the idea of it felt very North American, as if we were about to arrive at Coney Island. Faith warned me to curb my enthusiasm—it was just a wealthy town on the edge of the city.

We waited for the 501 streetcar for twenty minutes before Faith suggested we start walking. There had been more and more people gathering at the stop and now there was a pack. I could feel tension rising and the grumble of polite Canadians who were too frustrated and tired and late to tamp it down. Faith and I smiled at each other and started to move away from the crowd, down Queen Street towards the east. I took her hand, small and shy, and held it. It felt good to be out with her, and to show anyone who wanted to look what we were to each other.

We had been waiting in the part of Queen where it was mostly clothing stores and cafes, where people carrying bags of things they had already bought walked in and out of big loud shops flanked by bored security guards. I hadn't been inside H&M or Zara or Urban Outfitters but I had walked past them many times and seen the mannequins change outfits, from spring to summer, soon to fall.

I noticed as we walked that Faith didn't look in the windows, at the clothes on display or at her own reflection. I was always checking in the mirror of shop windows to get an idea of how terrible I looked or whether I needed to pat down my hair. She was compact and purposeful. It was calming.

After the shops we began to enter the neat beginning of Queen Street East where the Eaton Centre sat tall and clean on the left-hand side of the road. There were people everywhere—families spending their Saturday watching hockey players glide around Nathan Phillips Square on rollerblades, couples in matching shorts and singlets waiting for hot dogs at the vendors who always sat either side of Yonge Street. They had so many condiments hanging from their little carts that I had never attempted to order one. I would have wanted every topping—pickles, cheese, mustard, onions, those tasteless sliced black olives that were called Spanish olives in Australia, tomato sauce, shrivelled sauerkraut. I imagined that if Faith ordered one it would be plain, maybe covered with a thin trail of ketchup. I felt abundant around her, as if at any moment my indelicateness would become so evident she would shy away, and I'd never get to kiss her again.

I squeezed her hand and pointed out the dogs standing or sitting with their owners all over the place. Torontonians love dogs—the more eccentric the better. They were hot and tired and patient: small ones with big curls of frizzy yellow hair, big ones with black tongues and snake tails. We decided to pat any dog that came close, letting them sniff our hands first to show them we were safe.

As we crossed over Yonge Street and moved along Queen towards Church, there were fewer dogs. By the time we were at Jarvis there were no dogs at all, and at the front of Moss Park on our left we could see a group of men standing and one man on the ground beneath them. It was a park I'd been told not to walk through at night, and whenever I'd come down this way I'd seen unwell men and women, a completely different town to the one that only five minutes west was teeming with well-off people out for a nice time in the sun.

'Moss Park is absent from the psyche of so many people who love this city,' Faith said, as we waited to cross at the Jarvis Street lights. 'It's like we just close our eyes as the streetcar passes by this part.' She moved her hand to her hair and pushed it back, exposing a smooth forehead, lightly freckled. 'No one says anything, and everyone just keeps pretending that Toronto is perfect, and it doesn't change.'

I matched my steps with hers as we kept walking, slower now. It felt dangerous to be here, and I hated that I didn't seem to be able to push past that.

'I wonder why he's on the ground,' Faith said, looking over at the prone body. Her own was slightly tensed, and when the lights went green she walked quickly across and stood at the edge of the gutter so she could see better.

I joined her and could see that the man on the ground was moving slightly, kicking out at those who were standing above him. They were laughing, the men standing; the man on the ground wasn't, but he didn't seem distressed either. Then he pushed himself up to sitting and stood up, and he gave a few of the men standing a gentle punch on the arm. Faith's body became soft again. She looked at me and smiled, shrugging her small shoulders.

'I thought maybe he was in trouble,' she said quietly.

We kept walking, Faith with her head down. There was a hot wind coming at us along the pavement that brought the smell of something like rotting flowers, and I didn't know what to say. I looked over at her and saw that she was looking a little at me, with the corner of her face, her cheeks and neck a little pink.

'Sorry,' she said.

I didn't want her to think anything she did wasn't okay. 'Don't be sorry,' I said. 'Are you all right?'

She nodded and we walked a little faster, both of us at the same time, as if to move past whatever this was. I hadn't felt properly uncomfortable with Faith until that moment, and I remembered again she was a full and mysterious person, who held within her the possibility of breaking me apart and not making sense to me at any moment. I felt so scared that my hair bristled where it met my scalp, but I just continued to walk, and took her hand again, hoping mine wasn't shaking now. I decided then that I would go back into myself after the night. It wasn't worth it, this fear. We would just drift apart, and it would be expected, and I wouldn't have to worry about this anymore. It made the rest of the evening feel less daunting.

We were coming to the beginning of the Riverside Bridge, where you could turn left and enter the Distillery District. I had walked down there with Hetty soon after we arrived and we had sat at a cafe for as long as we could on the same margarita each. All the restaurants and bars in the area had seemed to serve only margaritas and oysters, and we could only afford one of one. It had been overcast that day, and Hetty had been wistful and slow: the beginning of her descent, it seemed now. I wondered what it would be like to tell Faith about how Hetty had been lately, and whether she would want to talk about it.

'My friend Hetty isn't going very well,' I said, starkly, as we stepped onto the arch of Riverside Bridge.

'Oh no,' Faith said, sounding concerned.

Ahead of us, above the bridge the words THIS RIVER I STEP IN IS NOT THE RIVER I STAND IN were written in curled capital letters. I said them inside my head. I didn't know quite how to explain what had been going on with Hetty, but I hoped it would help to tell someone.

'Yeah.' I stopped. Below us wasn't water, but just another road on a lower plane, I reminded myself.

'You know this bridge is just a road curved over another road?' I leaned over the side of the concrete barrier stopping us from walking off the edge. 'There's no water down there.'

Faith laughed. 'Tell me what's happening with Hetty,' she said.

I told her how Hetty had changed, and how much it seemed like she wasn't aware of it. I tried to explain that one of the ways she had changed was this lack of awareness, as if she no longer understood or cared how those who loved her felt, how she came across, what people thought or felt. I told her about the weight loss, the way she fell about when she was walking these days, how a couple of weeks ago she had thought she'd got a tattoo and all there had been was bare skin.

Faith took me seriously. She touched my shoulder and when a few tears popped out of my eyes she didn't turn hers away. I hoped as I talked, gasping a little, that it didn't seem strange that I was sad about what I was telling her, but of course Hetty and I were best friends and I had told Faith this, and of course she was gentle and nodding and asking and reasoning, and by the time we had reached the middle of Leslieville, hand in hand, I felt lighter. The tears dried quickly and I hoped they had blushed my cheeks rather than reddened my nose, and we stepped into a shop for ice cream that was full of dogs and children and well-dressed parents, where Faith ordered me a Rocky Road and I ordered her a Peanut Brittle.

She seemed to understand what was happening with Hetty, and communicated this to me quietly.

'She's not well,' Faith said, and took a small lick at her cone. She swallowed, dabbed at her mouth lightly with a serviette. 'Does she have a doctor?'

I wasn't sure, perhaps another sign that Hetty was slipping away from me, but I doubted that Hetty had a doctor in Toronto. She hadn't ever been good at looking after herself and never had any money. We didn't have health insurance, hadn't been in Ontario long enough to register for the generous health service. She would have had to be crawling from illness to book herself in.

'No, I don't think so.'
'Can you tell her? That you're worried?'
'I've tried.' I hadn't really tried. 'I'll try again.'
Faith's eyebrows lifted and she smiled at me. She leaned over

and kissed me on the lips, licking at the slick of ice cream there. My insides shook, down to my groin, then felt like they had been scooped out. I wanted to push her down onto the hot concrete and touch her under her dress with sticky fingers. There were too many friendly dogs, spoilt children, loving parents wearing new chinos and pressed shirts. I suggested we keep walking, and Faith nodded before I had even finished the sentence.

When we got to The Beaches the sky and the air were dull with heat and we ran straight up to the boardwalk and over towards the water to dip our toes in. It was so cold and my feet looked so big next to Faith's, but there was nothing to worry about. A group of people had spread out blankets against the sand and were playing music, and they weren't looking at us, so it felt private and full when Faith took my arm in hers and we stared out at the lake and the horizon.

It was beautiful here, and I understood why the rest of Toronto seemed almost to hate it, or to dismiss it, rolling their eyes at the name. They couldn't live here, because there weren't enough houses; the few houses were owned by people who had lots of money and were very lucky and probably thought they deserved more than one spare room, and that would make anyone hate anyone else. A part of me hoped I could come here again and again, but another part felt like I would never return.

We splashed each other for a while and then Faith swished her hair like a wet dog and suggested fish and chips. She said that she had only recently discovered that there was such a thing as fish and chips, had never imagined it could be acceptable to eat a fried meal out of a folded-over bit of butcher's paper. We waited at the shop in the electric light, then ate the halibut and chips and coleslaw on the sand. I told her about the devotion to fish and chips in Australia, along with deep-fried dim sims and tomato sauce, and battered saveloys. She started choking slightly, and I had to pat her back and give her water until it settled.

We didn't talk about Hetty again that day. It was dark and we were still sitting on the sand close to each other when we saw that there was really no one else around anymore—that we were alone. We edged closer to each other, my body aching, and then she moved so I was lying down with my hair in the sand and she was over me, on top of me, and we lapped against each other for not very long before I was breathless.

WETLAND
saturated land

I stayed at Faith's house after the beach and in the morning we woke up at almost the same time in her large lilac bed. She placed her hand down on me for a while, and then I could see her silky head there between my two legs, and I was nervous in a way that felt like floating. I could feel her tongue against my skin and we were both wetlands.

    Faith was so pretty that I didn't feel like I should do the same to her, until she asked me to with a big voice that I hadn't heard from her before. She smelt different to how she had smelt at the beach—she could open up to me properly there in her room, with the door closed and her bra around her belly where I had pulled it. I wanted to make her feel the way she was making me feel, and my stomach was hot against her thigh. She came quickly and with that same different voice telling me yes. Afterwards we lay on her pillows and I looked at her face with the light of the morning against it and let her look back at me, despite the fear.

Faith made toast in the kitchen for our afternoon tea when we finally stood, giggling at each other and our mussed hair and all the raw parts of us. There was a collection of small pots of jam on her counter—an orange one, a yellow one, a red one with pink at its bottom. She spread all our slices with lemon butter and put one in her mouth to carry our coffee to the rug at the edge of the floor.

I couldn't talk then because she was too perfect and I saw her little nude feet on the rug, and when I sat down mine were twice the size and had short hairs at their ends and I was not worthy of her at all, all of a sudden. I felt like a giant slug. I wondered whether it was normal to want to say *Thank you so much* and *Sorry, sorry, sorry* and *I'll go now—I'll never come back* to the woman you've just made love to.

She moved her head to the side as she watched me. 'You okay?'

'Not really,' I tried to joke, but it came out sounding like how I felt inside. Stewed and sad.

It was too bright and warm. I could feel the beginning of sweat on my upper lip and between my breasts, and I didn't want Faith to see it and regret ever touching me at all.

'I'm okay. I might have a shower,' I said, and pulled myself up to standing again. She looked up at me from way down on the rug, small and neat and worried.

'Ness, wait. Sit here with me while we eat,' she said, reaching out her arms and clasping my fingers with hers.

I sighed, and lowered myself down again. I felt scared now, as if everything could go away very quickly, and that I didn't deserve it to stay the way it was.

I sat looking at my hands, cross-legged with my feet under my thighs so Faith wouldn't have to see them. I could feel her watching my face and I felt as if I might cry, for no reason I could understand.

'Ness.'

She spoke softly and I felt her fingers against my arm, stroking at my paleness. I wished she would stop watching and touching, or that it was night again. It felt safer to be watched at night, because the shadows helped to hide some of me.

I hated feeling like this, and remembered why I'd never wanted a girlfriend in the first place. It was disgusting, sitting there feeling so big and cornered. I knew now it wouldn't be long until she would reject me with her quiet kindness. It wasn't her fault I couldn't maintain things because I was too rough, too scared. I wished it was men I felt this way around, instead of women. When I was with a man I didn't care what my body looked like, or whether I was slick or red or smelly. I just wanted to find any pleasure I could from the encounter and leave without thought. Women meant more, so much more.

I turned to her and let my face open. Maybe I could just tell her I was scared. I'd never done that before. She was the kindest and this the loveliest moment, after all.

'I'm scared that if you see me in the light you won't want me anymore,' I said. I wiped the back of my hand, finally, against my upper lip and then my chin. The beads of sweat transferred from skin to skin. I hoped my face wasn't red.

Faith's eyes turned down. 'No!' she said. 'Oh. Ness. No.'

'Sorry,' I said, my lips hardly moving.

It was tiring being vulnerable and raw. I wished myself anywhere else, anywhere else alone, anywhere else where she wasn't, so I could be huge and ugly and sad without her beautiful eyes seeing me.

She sighed, and took my hand and put one hand on top of it and one hand underneath it and pressed lightly with each of them. 'You don't need to say sorry, or be sorry. Thank you for telling me how you're feeling.'

I stayed looking down, at my hand in between hers.

'It's how you feel now, but it's not real, Ness. I am incredibly attracted to every part of you.'

I could feel her breath, her face and mouth close to my neck by then.

She kissed my neck and each cheek. 'That part and this part,' she said, then kissed my forehead. 'And this part'—lifting my arm up from where it was pulled close against my side and kissing deep against my armpit. I let myself feel her lips and not worry about what she was touching when she touched me with them.

'And these parts,' she said again, and kissed little kisses down the side of me and in, to my belly button.

'Faith, you don't have to,' I said.

She shushed me and kept kissing until she was at my vagina, and I let her show me over and over.

TRIBUTARY
a river feeding a river

After summer had opened up into autumn, everything changed in a rush. Hetty didn't come home one Friday night and then the Saturday night, and she wasn't answering her phone when I called it after wondering whether I should let her be. When I went to Ronnie's on Sunday afternoon to find her, she wasn't there, though she always had a shift on Sundays. Elaine was behind the soggy-carpeted bar when I arrived, wiping glasses with a tea towel that looked too wet to do the job, and she didn't smile. I wished I hadn't, then told her I was looking for Hetty.

'She didn't come in for work yesterday.' Elaine turned around to begin moving the glasses she had dried to the shelf.

'Is she supposed to be here today?'

I couldn't believe Hetty hadn't come in for a shift and that Elaine wasn't even going to stand there and talk to me about why this might be, without me having to beg her to.

'Yeah, but I'm not holding my breath,' she said, banging

down a crate of pint glasses covered in shadows of beer froth.

'Well, where is she?'

My heart was beating fast in anger. Elaine was supposed to be Hetty's friend. This bar, this person, were such unsafe things for her to try to build her life around, and I'd known that. I should have been making sure she was okay.

'I have no idea. Her phone's off now. I really don't have time for this, Ness. I'm understaffed.'

I hadn't even thought she would remember my name. Her voice saying it made me feel strange, like she was family, despite her being nothing to me, or Hetty. She had her back to me again, was washing something under the tap, when I turned myself around and walked out, though I'd wanted to ask her if she had noticed Hetty's behaviour lately. She didn't know Hetty anyway—there was no point. She was angry and she'd given up on her.

Outside on the street I remembered that it was the weekend and took in a breath of smoke from a barbecue that was selling sausages and the sweat of people walking their weeks off. I didn't know what to do next. I hadn't met any of Hetty's other new friends—had just heard tiny things about them over and over, like how Jeff liked silent discos and Freya had a problem with sleeping unless she smoked weed. I didn't know where they would be, or how to find out. Hetty was far away from me now, and I didn't know how to get her back.

I walked home and found Steph and Robin in the kitchen, talking with cups of coffee in hand, and Whitney asleep on the table atop a pile of newspapers. They told me they hadn't seen Hetty since earlier that week, and that Dill was in his room, so I climbed the stairs and knocked on his bedroom door, painted lemon yellow with a photo of Whitney in a basket stuck to it with sticky tape. I heard him call out, and then he was there, with the door open, and the smell of marijuana, and a look of something on his face, and I asked if I could talk to him. We sat on his bed, cross-legged, facing one another. I hadn't been in there before, in Dill's room. It was carefully decorated and neat.

'I don't know where Hetty is,' I told him, and watched his freckled face as he ran his hand through his hair. His eyes were red. I felt myself on the verge of crying, and tried to swallow it down.

'Is she at work?'

I shook my head.

'Sorry—of course you would have checked that first. When did you last see her?'

I pictured the last time in my mind. Tuesday that week, in the morning. Me creeping around the bedroom trying to find a clean top, trying not to wake her. She was asleep on her side of the bed but almost on my side too—her long hair spread across the cotton and almost black in the white morning light, her face squished in between the place where our pillows met. I hadn't been awake the night before when she'd got home, but the air was slightly muggy with the smell of wine and skin, and I had assumed she was very hungover. She hadn't stirred, and I had left for work.

'Tuesday morning. But that's not so weird. Sometimes I don't see her for ages. It's just that she's not answering her phone and she missed work yesterday and Elaine doesn't know where she is.' I paused. 'I just have a bad feeling.'

Dill nodded and sighed.

'Are you stoned, by the way? Sorry if I interrupted some kind of Sunday session...'

Dill laughed, and rubbed at his face with his sturdy fingers.

'Yeah, a little. But don't worry! It's good you came to tell me.'

I could see now that he was a bit slower than usual in his movements and speech. Usually an energy was in the air just around him and he was almost visibly trying to take the edge off his own pace, his own excitement. Today he was moving through mud.

'When did you last see her?'

He looked up at the ceiling, eyes pinky red, remembering.

'I saw her on Wednesday,' he said, his voice firm. 'She was having a drink before she went to work. I asked her how she was and she started crying.'

He stopped and looked at me, waiting for my reaction, but I didn't say anything. I wanted to hear more.

'I hoped I'd see her this weekend to talk to her more. She didn't have time to tell me what was wrong then, and I didn't ask the right questions, I don't think.'

I could hear the gulp in his voice. My heart hurt picturing Hetty pouring herself a mug of wine with tears in her eyes, hoping to numb something. That pale, bare small of back beneath her clothes. I was sure though that Dill would have been gentle, kind, open to talking, and that Hetty would have known she could have asked to tell him anything. If Dill was the last kind person she had seen since then, at least she had seen him.

'I'm sure she knew she could talk to you.'

Dill smiled and nodded. It was comfortable sitting there on his bed, with his silvery doona beneath us and a fug of smoke settling in the air. I could feel that Dill was sad just like Hetty was, but that he knew how to be with sadness. It wasn't lonely in that room, and I felt a rare moment of ease in the company of someone else.

Dill tried to call Hetty's phone then, and this time it didn't even ring, just went straight to her calm, sweet voicemail. I called her from my phone, just to see, and it did the same. Her voice was lighter and higher on the recording than when she was right there with me. I wanted to see her. I wanted to give her a hug and hold her thin body against mine.

Dill had met a friend of Hetty's from Ronnie's a few weeks earlier when he'd visited her there one afternoon to say hello.

'It was this guy called Rick, and he was a complete jerk.'

This didn't surprise me. Hetty often found herself surrounded by jerks and never seemed to see quite how unpleasant they were. She sometimes made dumb choices when it came to people, in the name of tenderness and hark, and forgave much too easily. I had talked to her so many times about how important it was for her to value the friendship she gave to people, to make sure she didn't empty all of it out on the wrong ones. She would never quite understand, but would tell me that I was the only one who mattered. I let it go mostly, though with Sean I hadn't been able to and it had nearly destroyed us.

'The jerks always find her.'

I told Dill about Elaine, and how her vibe was pit-bull demon and she clearly didn't give a shit about Hetty even after all the time they'd spent together, and how angry that made me. I could feel my body warming when I thought about how much Hetty gave to some people and how little she got back. Dill raised his eyebrows, then he got angry too. I loved him for it.

'So Elaine has no idea where Hetty might be?'

'I didn't even really ask her. She was too busy cleaning the bar to properly talk to me. She was more upset about Hetty missing her shift.'

Dill sighed, pressed a hand on top of mine briefly.

'I just wonder whether people are drawn to her fragility and then repelled by it, you know?'

I knew.

'And like, nothing touches her, but also everything does?'

He moved across the bed and put his arm down towards the carpet below, bringing up a small wooden box with a carved lid. He took out papers and a bud waiting green in a small bowl, and started chopping at it with scissors.

'That's exactly what it is. She's weird.'

By weird, I meant loveable and unique and undone, and I knew Dill knew that. We shared the joint lying on his pillows, which were smooth and smelt of lavender detergent: the big box of it we had in the laundry that seemed to last forever. He rolled onto his side and watched me as I took a drag.

'So we will have to go find her?'

'Yes,' I answered, smoke coming out of my open mouth like a rain cloud. I heard Whitney scratching quietly at the door. Dill told me gently that he knew where Rick lived. We edged ourselves up and put our shoes on.

~

It was warm outside, with a woozy wind.

Dill told me that when he'd met Rick at Ronnie's, Hetty had seemed to know him well. I'd never heard Hetty say Rick's name, but that didn't mean much. She got to know people quickly, or at least the surface of them. People made her their best friend in minutes, and she never told them she was taken.

We walked up Spadina and turned right, towards Dundas and College and after that Bloor, towards the university and the area of Toronto known as the Annex, where young people and middling families lived in a semi-boho funk.

Dill said that Rick had been talking about his new place, and had told Hetty and Dill he'd moved into a share house just off Bloor that was painted purple, with two women and a dog called Guy. Dill had known as soon as Rick said the house was purple and the dog was Guy that it was the house his friend Shauna lived in, and told Rick this, with astonishment, even camaraderie in his tone. Rick's response had been blank, as if he didn't care and wasn't sure why Dill had even mentioned it. This was when Dill knew that he didn't like Rick, and he had told Hetty he would catch up with her at home.

'So unless he's moved out, or Shauna has decided she doesn't want to live with him after all, that's where he lives. In the crazy purple house. Guy is a chihuahua, by the way.'

We laughed at the little dog's name, and as we neared Dundas I could smell oyster sauce and vegetables. My stomach and my mouth and my chest were sick again from the weed and the heat and the not knowing where Hetty was, and reminding myself she was probably not going well, if she'd missed work and couldn't charge her phone, and hadn't been able to tell me anything. Shivers filled me, despite the hot sun.

I looked over at Dill, who was so gorgeous and reliable and Canadian, and I felt homesick. Not just for Melbourne or the familiar, but for when I was just a little younger and when I hadn't moved to the other side of the world and when life had surely been easier.

The wind was picking up as if it had a fan behind it, helping it to blaze through and beyond. We passed College Street and walked around one side of the big roundabout that came before Bloor. Dill tried calling Hetty again, and it was just her recorded voice telling us her phone was still off. I could hear a tiny part of her coming out of the speaker at Dill's ear.

'Hetty. Dill again. Ness and I are worried about you. Please call us back.'

Dill's phone voice was the same as his normal one, and this felt reassuring in that moment. I was out of breath from the very gradual hill we were climbing: my heart burned. My body seemed to be remembering the other times in my life that I had thought Hetty was lost to me.

CREEK
a small stream

When we were both twenty, Hetty and I went to stay on a farm about an hour's drive north-west of Melbourne. Hetty and Sean hadn't been talking for weeks—they were on a break that I hoped would last forever—and she'd asked me if I would come with her to stay in a house on a farm that had within its boundaries a small school run by the author of young-adult books that were popular when we were growing up. The school was deliberately separate from the mainstream, and the pupils were treated like budding creative scholars with things to offer and a capacity to learn about the land. We would help out with the running of the place and stay in the old farmhouse for free, and it seemed like the right time for me to do something, anything, and for Hetty to get away.

We drove there in my white Corolla, coated with a reddy-brown dust by the time we arrived, and played Laura Marling down low on the broken stereo, which I remember felt comforting. Hetty was hopeful that this time away in the bush would help her decide what to do with her life and about Sean, and I wanted to join her.

When we arrived it seemed as if nobody had been expecting us. It was a beautiful hilled property, with the school in a small domed building up near the highest part. The farmhouse we would be staying in was to the side and we were guided there by a man called Cliff, who was too tall and had the quietest voice—as if he was telling us secrets. He helped us with our bags across the creek, showed us to our little rooms side by side, and then he left, telling us we could get a lift to town later to pick up groceries for our dinner, if we needed.

There didn't seem to be a kitchen, but eventually we found it: a small separate room, clinging like a clam to the side of the hill. We were so hungry we didn't feel fussy. I found some spaghetti in a cupboard and boiled it with salt and margarine from an old fridge for us to eat. Out on the verandah, sunk in to a comfortable outside couch with a bowl full of golden noodles, I was glad to be there. It smelt like cut grass and scraps, and there was a hog watching us from across the garden, his thick body dirty behind a wire fence.

We found out the next morning that the hog's name was Bill. He was businesslike when we went to feed him—a big bucket of half-finished yesterday's lunch from the school and some spotty bananas—and immediately began huffing it down with his tiny tail wiggling. I wanted to pat the white-pink-dust hairy skin of his back, but I had been told once that hogs could be vicious, even though this didn't seem likely now that I had met one. Hetty leaned over and ruffled his big ears. He ignored her entirely. Cliff was with us, and he whispered words of encouragement to Bill across the fence as he ate.

We had woken early that first day, and once dressed had wandered up to the school and found ourselves in the midst of morning-tea prep—a kitchen full of sturdy women in aprons slapping buttered bread slices upon buttered bread slices onto laminex benchtops. Hetty hadn't seemed fazed. She told the sturdiest woman who we were and why we were there, and the woman introduced herself to us as Belle. She told us she supposed we should meet with the author, David, and took us out of the main dining area and across a bit of grass to another, smaller building.

It was strange, knowing we were about to meet the man who had written books I had read over and over when I was younger, someone I had imagined to be so mysterious and intelligent that he couldn't possibly be living a life I could see for myself. After Belle knocked on the door we waited, and then she knocked again. I looked across at Hetty as we stood there and noticed she was standing tall and serious, her face poised.

Just as Belle raised her small red fist to knock again, the door opened. The man standing there was tall and grey, with strong shoulders. He wore a red wool jumper full of holes and jeans, and behind him I could see rows and rows of books on shelves, from the floor to the ceiling. He smiled lightly, as if he understood something beyond us, and as Belle told him who we were I watched his face move to say hello. There was an air of quiet to him in that moment that stayed, despite how much we went on to talk to him and to hear him talk, despite all his words.

Hetty shook his hand too long and stared—I remember that

because he commented on it, gently, and we laughed. He thanked Belle and she left to get started on 'lunch for the ratbags'. I felt their personalities separate against each other as she left and started across the flat ground towards the kitchen. She was no-nonsense in her capability and foresight, her face like the dawn sun. He was complex and faltered against his own darkness.

~

We did all sorts of things during those few weeks. Pulling weeds, mixing cakes, sitting in the nurse's station with the delicately injured children while she had her lunchbreak, watching for brown snakes as we mowed the angry grass. I drove us around and up and down bump-hills in the ATV, with Hetty hanging on behind me, her warm arms wrapped around my stomach, my heartbeat a little quick. We picked apricots and plums in the orchard, and ate too many; we lay around in the library after all the kids had gone home, letting the cool air indulge us as we read and rested. We talked to each other, as we always did, and were free with our thoughts about the place and what was happening there.

    A tiny school for children whose parents wanted a different sort of education for them—a special one. A teacher who seemed to understand young people in the way he wrote and spoke, as if he wasn't that far away from that time in his own life, though he was. A thick bush surround, with creek maps. I told Hetty I wondered if David was too critical of mainstream education, that it might be a bad thing that he wasn't open to it, that his vision was idealistic and inaccessible. Hetty disagreed in her easy way and told me she thought he was the realistic one.

I got very sunburnt one afternoon a few days before we were leaving and had to go to bed early, placing a wet towel over my red chest and naked body, with the fan on and near. I felt sick and thirsty, and wished I was back in Melbourne, where there was less dark and more noise outside the windows. Hetty decided she would go alone to a dinner that David had invited us to—after I insisted over and over that I would be fine—and I was sad to see her go. It was at the house of a friend of David's who also taught at the school, and we had been so excited to be asked, feeling it was confirmation that David liked us and thought we were interesting. I see now he was likely being polite, and using the dinner invitation as a way of thanking us for our time on the farm, but we were hopeful back then, and unsure of our worth, and this edged our minds towards the grandiose.

After she had left, dressed in a linen shift with nectarine lipstick, I tried to rest. It was a slow night and I woke often, getting up to let my bladder loose of the large amounts of water I had drunk to ward off heatstroke, noticing each time that Hetty hadn't returned yet. Her bedroom door was wide open and the light of the moon made her untidy bed glow. It looked so empty without her long, edged body. I didn't worry, because I was too hot and sore and tired.

I woke early in the morning and pricked my ears to hear Hetty in the next room, snoring, but there was nothing. When I got out of bed, slowly to avoid the crinkling of my damaged skin, and went to check, she was still not there. I wondered who I could check with, who might know where she was, and whether it was too early to do so. Outside the grass was dewy and I could see Bill behind the fence sleeping in a dried-up mud bath, his fleshy face slack against the dirt. I didn't know where I was going, but walking up the hill towards the school felt purposeful, and I could see people rushing around preparing for the new day, which eased my anxiety.

No one in the kitchen area or the eating area or the nursing area had seen Hetty. I kicked at grass and walked around the grassy hill behind the main building deciding what to do, and could only think of the author, David, and how he had seen her last, at the dinner, and how he would be the one to know where she was, if anyone did. It didn't feel right to go and knock at his office door, as we had done on the first day with the support of Belle, but I couldn't think of anything else that would be easier, or more helpful, and I reasoned that he would probably not even be in there yet.

It was still early, and there were still signs of dew. No children had arrived for their day yet, and breakfast was still a plan in Belle's head rather than a pile of egg sandwiches. I carefully moved myself down towards David's office, making sure to go slow and sideways like a crab. It was slippery and steep, and I was sleepy.

He answered his door almost as soon as I had finished quietly knocking. He was smiling in his knowing way, and beckoned me in before I could tell him I was there to find Hetty. Further inside was stacked with books—piles and piles of them hiding other piles, a bookshelf absolutely crammed. They were teetering and worn, well loved.

'I'm looking for Hetty,' I told David after he had asked me how I was, and I had politely answered.

He raised his eyebrows and laughed, took his glasses off and looked to be wiping at one of his eyes.

'Hetty? She not back yet?'

He told me that she had stayed on at his friend's place after dinner, too tired to journey back to the farm and not able to get to the car for a lift with David and his wife. I understood this to mean she had been drunk, and I pictured her sleeping on a couch in an imagined house, with big windows and tall gums watching her from outside.

David smiled a small smile and told me not to worry. It had been a pleasant evening; she would be back soon; his friend would give her a lift as soon as she woke. I cringed for her inside, and made myself laugh lightly, to make sure it was nothing. Hetty drank when she was nervous—more than me because it gave her pluck rather than a muddy head. I hoped she hadn't lost herself.

That evening, after Hetty had returned and recounted, with lifted shoulders, details about David's friend's house and the meal they had eaten and the way she had woken up without any memory of why she was there, arms covered in thin sleep lines from lying in one place too long, we ate eggs on toast on the verandah and swatted the mozzies away. I made mine into a sandwich, and Hetty sliced hers up into tiny yolky squares, and I let the feeling of her next to me make me happy, as I often did. She didn't apologise for scaring me. I liked it that way. We laughed at Bob snuffling some banana peels and planned our trip home along the Ring Road.

KETTLE
formed by retreating glaciers

Dill and I arrived at the purple house as the light was dusking into pink behind the clouds. It was just off Bloor Street West in the middle of the Annex, and looked like a giant piece of iced gingerbread, complete with musk-stick pillars either side of the porch.

We had stopped talking for the last part of the walk—both of us retreating inward to our own versions of Hetty, to our own versions of what might have kept her away for the last few days. I wanted her to be inside that house so badly, and I performed the superstitious ritual I had been compulsively doing since I was young: crossing my fingers and my toes as we waited at the door, closing my eyes just briefly, telling whoever could hear me that this wish was important.

The door was opened by a woman about our age with short blond hair in a grown-out pixie cut curled around her ears. Dill exclaimed, and I knew it must be Shauna. A small dog came running up to the doorway, yapping and skitting on its tiny paws. I felt I should say hello and pat Guy but I didn't particularly want to—the dog was so skinny its eyes were popping out of its skull and it appeared to be agitated. Shauna gave Dill a long, clinging hug, acknowledged me in a tired way and led us into the house to show us to Rick's room.

I had expected the inside of the house to resemble the outside, but just as the human skin hides something else entirely, the walls of the place were tastefully cream and the furniture plain and comforting. I was relieved. Hetty hated the colour purple—had said many times it reminded her of her inevitable future, of purple smocks and purple hair and purple dangly parrot earrings—and I didn't want to know she had been lying around in it, letting it seep into her skin.

We ended up down the back of the house, where a staircase was hiding between bits of wall. Shauna told us to climb to the top and knock at the door there; she didn't seem to want to take us up, to be engaged in anything any longer, and she left us, telling Dill to text her, which he agreed to, and looking at me one more time with her clouded eyes. Dill and I glanced at each other, our eyebrows raised, and he shrugged and gave a small laugh. I wanted to ask him if Shauna was always so vague, but I couldn't find a better word and I felt like there was history there, between them, and that Dill wouldn't want to be cruel.

'Shall we?' Dill said, and gestured up the stairs with his hand.

'Oh, please, after you.' I gestured back. I didn't want to be the one to knock on Rick's door, to be the face that he saw first when he opened it. Dill would be much better at explaining that we were just worried, and if Hetty was there, he wouldn't overreact. I needed to stand back and breathe deeply.

He winked at me, smiled with all his perfect teeth. 'She'll be okay, you know.'

After Dill knocked and we stood perched on the top step waiting, I could hear a shuffling and a murmuring and the shifting of at least one body. Dill and I looked at the wood we were standing on and listened, but there were no more noises. Then a loud voice asked, 'What?'

I answered back, my heart fast, wanting this to be over. 'Hi, Rick, we're looking for Hetty. It's her friends Ness and Dill!'

The brightness in my voice surprised me. I wanted Rick to give her up.

We waited, my palms damp with anxiety, Dill wiping the back of his hand across his upper lip. It was hot and close.

'Hang on,' the loud voice said.

The door jutted open, the wood shrieking, as if it was hardly ever required to perform such a task. I could immediately smell grass, and ashtray, and spray deodorant, all three scents equally overwhelming. Rick was standing tall, hair in eyes, no shirt on, one hand on a slim hip. He was Hetty's type—the wrong type that she often chose. He was almost leaning back into the air around him, boyishly thin.

He turned away and pushed the door open wider, nudging at the darkness behind him with his head.

'She's sleeping.'

I couldn't see anything in the space behind him, but my eyes began to adjust as I entered. Through the thick air I could see that the room was spacious, and there was a couch and a large bed with messy sheets across it, and in the middle of the bed was a length that was Hetty. I blinked and leaned forward: she was curled up with her thighs against her chest, almost kissing her own knees, like she did when she was cold or sad. I breathed all the air out of my tummy and murmured thank you to something.

Dill was next to me, and when Rick moved aside he walked past me and towards the mattress.

'Hetty?' he whispered.

I watched Rick, who was still standing and still had his hair in his eyes.

'I'm Hetty's best friend,' I said to the growth of him, to his long spine and his bony boy fingers.

He didn't respond.

'Is she okay?'

Rick clicked his tongue, still staring straight ahead from behind his hair, at nothing. 'She's fine. We just had a big one last night, eh.'

Dill looked over at me from where he stood beside the bed.

'She's just sleeping,' he said, in a quiet voice that reminded me this would be hard for him.

All the anger I hadn't been allowing myself caught fire in me then. Hetty wasn't okay; she wasn't communicating; she was asleep in a nasty man's bed; she was curled up the way she curled up when she didn't feel good. I couldn't go and lie next to her, because it wasn't our bed and she didn't even know that I was there, and I felt like crying and hitting this idiot in the stomach and any place I could get him for taking her away. I tried to douse it, the reality of what was happening to us, but it just stayed there, aflame, and so I asked Dill if we could leave.

'She obviously doesn't care anyway,' I said to no one as we stepped carefully down the wooden stairs.

Dill answered me, 'She does, Ness, she does,' and the tears came out of my eyes then because he might have been wrong.

SEEP
formed by a spring

Faith and I had breakfast together the next morning. Hetty hadn't come home that night and I had tried to enjoy having the bed to myself, stretching out and leaving my book beside me on top of the doona when my eyes started to droop, but it hadn't made me feel any better. I was still angry, and it felt like I was about to choke when I thought about how much things had changed between Hetty and me, slowly but surely and then all of a sudden, since we had arrived. The leaves swishing outside our window, on a stage lit by the street lamps, seemed cruel as I lay there. I wished they were gum leaves.

Faith had her hair plaited and the plait circled her face. Even though I felt sick from residual anxiety about Hetty, I ordered a pile of maple-syrup pancakes with blueberries and banana, and we shared them, cutting through the layers side by side.

'It's so nice to see you,' I told her. 'You look really beautiful.'

She leaned towards me around the side of the table, small smile and pale-pink lips lined like shells. She reached out to hold my face with both her little hands and kissed it all over, all down my nose and along each cheek to my forehead. My pelvis and kidneys and lungs burned for more of her. I didn't care that there were people at every table around us who had only just realised we were lovers and not friends, and that their faces would probably show me how they felt about that. I didn't look and I didn't care.

'It's so nice to see you too,' she said.

She poked her fork into a slice of banana and brought it to her mouth, licking at the sides as she chewed and swallowed.

I wanted to tell her about Hetty, and Dill and me trying to find her, and the circle of her body on the dirty bed, but when I tried to work out how to explain how sad it made me that she was there with a man like Rick, as if time had sucked itself in and popped itself back out from the beginning, I couldn't think of the words.

'So, you found her. Where was she?'

I had texted Faith when I got home from the purple house, leaving Dill with Robin and Steph and Clark and Ingrid in the kitchen to climb the stairs and lie down. I'd told her Hetty was okay, that she was safe, and that I had seen her to make sure. No other way of telling had come to me, as I kicked my shoes off and lowered my body onto the cool covers. I'd turned my phone off after sending it too, to dull any extra sensation, to black myself out. Faith's reply had blinked at me in the morning when I turned it back on. *Oh, thank goodness. Thank goodness. x*

'She was at some guy's house. Rick.' The name dug at my stomach. 'She was asleep in his room, on this big bed. All curled up.'

Faith's face crinkled and she took my hand.

'Oh, Ness. I wish she'd told you where she was. Did you get to speak to her?'

'No.'

The word was choked and I worried I was about to cry again. I didn't want to start crying in the cafe and make my face all red and snotty.

'I just felt so angry.'

'Of course you did,' Faith said.

'Anyway. I don't want to spend all our time together talking about Hetty.'

Faith laughed. 'Neither do I!'

She looked at me carefully and put her arms on the table in front of her, leaning forward a little in a way that almost didn't suit her.

'Do you think Hetty is beautiful?' she asked.

I had known this would come eventually. I had imagined my response and hadn't been able to think of something that didn't sound false, or inadequate. I couldn't say no; I couldn't say yes—*but you are much more*. I couldn't get upset that we were having this conversation now, when I knew why she was asking me.

She was waiting for me to answer, with a clear face and no lines. I took a breath but only from my chest, not my stomach. I couldn't pull the air down to there.

'Do you?'

'I asked you,' she replied evenly.

I sighed so she could hear me. It wasn't fair, but I did it. A sigh could tell her that it was pointless to go where we were going, and encourage her not to go there again.

'Yes, Hetty's beautiful. She's not as beautiful as you, though.'

Faith's eyes were still on me too much. It felt near the edge of painful. 'I don't care about that. I'd rather be free than beautiful.'

'What do you mean?'

'She's so lost. It's like she's playing a part in a sad indie film. Hoping everyone will fall in love with her so she won't have to stand up on her own.'

I felt my love for Hetty in my chest, where it always was, and at Faith's comment it roared like a cub. Of course she was jealous—I would be. The deeper Hetty sunk, the deeper I would stretch out my hand for her. It was so obvious, despite all the energy I used up trying to hide it.

I couldn't open that window so Faith could see in, though. It was the part of me she wouldn't be able to live with, and I couldn't work out how to give it up.

'That's not fair, Faith.'

I don't know if there were tears in the corners of her eyes but her neck was red by then, plotted with rash circles, and she told me she had to go. The tight loyalty in my chest kept me from asking her to stay, or admitting defeat, but I wanted to run out of the cafe after she had walked out the door like I was in a cheesy movie and yell for her to come back. There wouldn't be any words I'd need to say but she'd know what I wanted, and it was her. We'd kiss in front of everyone and there would be clapping.

Instead I sat there, and when a waiter came by I asked for the bill.

That afternoon I walked around, not wanting to go back to Marjorie and not wanting to sit down anywhere and be still with myself.

Toronto seemed to be full of joy. As I walked along Ossington I looked for someone else walking on their own and couldn't find anyone. There were couples and families with prams and pinwheel hats and ice cream, and groups of friends laughing at themselves in a way that made my whole torso throb to be feeling the way they were feeling.

I didn't miss Melbourne, not really, because if I imagined myself there I saw myself doing the same thing. I was losing Hetty, and I had lost the one girl who had ever wanted to kiss me when she was sober, and I didn't have anyone I could call. The only thing that seemed slightly positive was that if I kept walking, maybe I would shake something off; maybe the part of me that never got things right would get too tired and die, leaving a shell I could fill with other people's qualities. My body was blue then—I could see it along my arms and in my fingers, despite the autumn sun—but moving felt like it could take the cold away, so I kept going.

I decided to move towards another part of the city. I hadn't been up past Bloor Street to Bloordale, but had heard from Dill and Robin that it was a place you could walk around and feel like you were in a different time, somewhere small and slow and serious where marble fountains in front gardens and Our Lady of Lourdes statues stood curved and proud, dry and slightly damaged.

There wasn't so much joy as I crossed over Lansdowne and

entered Bloordale. The people walking here were older, more grey in their hair and their skin, and they had a purpose or conviction that made me feel as if it wasn't the weekend here like it was further downtown, or that these people had responsibilities beyond a working week. There was no ambling, just the shuffle of older legs and tired feet on concrete.

Most of the people were on their own like me, and I finally let my shoulders down. I could imagine what it would be like up here in the winter and maybe even what it would be like after it snowed, white covering all the surfaces of each tiny house, the small sidewalks swept for those who could get themselves out. I remembered what Faith had said about Bloordale—that she knew I would like it, and that she knew that because it was odd and modest and yet proud in its own way, just like me.

I walked slowly through the quiet and thought about what Faith had said about Hetty, and how much more she must have felt that she hadn't yet said, and how much I regretted telling her it wasn't fair when I knew it was fair and she was so gracious. I thought these thing and sighed, feeling the regret seep through me. I knew too that she had been telling the truth when she said she would rather be free than beautiful, though she was both.

Ruining this, this thing we had had, had been my destiny. There was no point being disappointed. I couldn't maintain Faith. She was above and beyond and outside of me, even when I had had my fingers inside of her and had made her whine down to the bottom of her throat.

SOUND
deeper than a bight, wider than a fjord

When I finally headed home to Marjorie it was past dinnertime and I could see lights on inside from down the street as I got closer.

Steph and Robin were in the kitchen, which was soft yellow and smelt like oranges. It was very cold that night, though it was still only autumn, still fall, and they were making mulled wine on the old brown stove. I took a mugful and they asked me to sit.

'Are you okay, Ness?' Robin asked, turning towards me with his slight face.

The fatigue rushed up and I started to cry. I felt Steph take my cup and Robin come up to rub my back, and heard Whitney mewling below me.

'Hetty's upstairs,' Steph said from above me.

It was a shock to hear she was back. I had imagined she would stay at Rick's for days, too ashamed or sick or apathetic to make the journey back to us. Robin and Steph knew Hetty had been struggling, and I wondered what she'd said to them when she got back, if anything.

I looked up through the wet of my tears and saw them both half-standing, half-crouched, hovering for me. It felt good—they were such good people. I hoped they didn't regret letting us live with them.

'She seemed okay, you know. Just so you know,' Robin told me.

'Thanks,' I said.

I didn't want to go up and find her. We sat, and I felt the tears dry on my face and my cheeks shrink slightly from the salt, and Robin poured more steaming wine into his cup and told us about the new guy at his work who had asked him out for coffee. Everyone wanted to have coffee with Robin. He was so pretty and delightful. I imagined kissing him and tasted the memory of honey. The wine warmed my hands but I didn't want to drink it. Hetty was probably drunk up there, lying on our bed with one long leg crossed over another, wishing she was somewhere else. For once, it felt pathetic to try to join her.

'Let's go to Sneak's,' Steph said.

Sneak's was Sneaky Dee's: a tacky Mexican cafe with five-dollar breakfasts and two-dollar beers that stayed open late and had a dance floor upstairs that nearly broke through the ceiling every Saturday night. I had been there with Hetty soon after we had arrived and it had been boiling in the small room that held the dance floor above the stairs. Hetty's face had shone as she bounced up and down, her hair flicking at me and sticking to my chest when she twisted. I'd vomited in a gutter on the way back to Jo's and we'd laughed, arms over shoulders, at the mess of ourselves. Maybe it would be good to go there again and shake off some of the loss that was clinging to me.

I realised then that they were both quite drunk, the heat of it coming off them. Steph's eyes flicked from Robin to me as she tipped her cup up into her mouth. Robin pulled me up and danced me across the floor.

'Hey, Ness,' I heard from behind me as Robin tipped me down towards the ground and pulled me back up to swing me out again.

Hetty was standing at the entrance of the kitchen. She looked tired and tall and very thin, and her hair was looped up above her head and pinned so it looked like a private nest. She was instantly familiar.

We stepped towards each other and moved into a hug and I felt her neck cool against my cheek. She put her hands on my shoulders, moved me back and looked at me, as if she hadn't seen me in so long, which she hadn't, and as if I was worth seeing again. I watched her face through the wool of hair which had fallen across mine. She was smiling and crying. She always cried.

'I'm so sorry I haven't checked in.'

I didn't want to say that it was okay, but I hadn't had any practice telling Hetty things she didn't want to hear.

'You don't have to say it's okay. I know it's not okay.' She pushed my hair back, tapped her finger against my nose. 'How are you?'

I didn't want to talk about how I'd lost Faith before I'd even really had her or how I was exhausted from worrying about Hetty being in some unmoved jerk's room curled up like a scared child or how I wanted to leave Toronto because it felt like I'd never be a part of the city but I'd never felt a part of Melbourne either or that I was truly wondering what the point of anything was, really.

'I'm all right,' I said.

'Ness...'

I turned to see if Robin and Steph were listening. They were standing next to each other at the stove, Robin stirring the saucepan of wine, Steph leaning against him.

I turned back to Hetty, who was looking at me, waiting. 'I don't want to talk about anything, Het.'

She sighed and pulled her jumper sleeves down to cover the whole of her arms. 'Rick told me you and Dill came to see me.'

I pictured Rick sitting on that bed next to Hetty after she had finally woken up, telling her with his hard voice that two of her weird friends had knocked on his door asking for her. There was something about him that made me wonder what he'd done in his life, and how bad it had been. And that bed had been so grimy.

'We came to see if you were there because we didn't know where you were. You missed work and weren't answering your phone. If you hadn't been at Rick's I would have had to call the police.'

I didn't want her to feel guilty but I didn't want her to do it again either. I knew that since we were little I'd given Hetty more kindness than was good for her. It was almost like it had turned her into a spoilt child.

'Why did you do that? What happened?' I asked, my voice louder now.

She was looking down, at the floorboards or at her feet with their chipped yellowed nails. People like Hetty didn't have to make sure they cleaned themselves up so that people wouldn't think them lazy or ugly. The world thought them exceptional and beautiful anyway.

'Hetty!'

I was sick of her avoiding everything. It hurt me too much and it was selfish. Her family had given her safety in numbers. Over here she only had me, and she was neglecting that.

'Sorry. I don't know,' she answered finally, her voice a small bird in a high tree.

'You don't know?'

'No. I'm sorry.'

I turned away from her and walked towards Robin and Steph. 'Are we going out?' I said.

They were excited, the two of them, and they jumped and clapped a little. We got ready quickly, leaving Hetty to stand where she had been standing looking at the floor and then move to the couch in the living room, where she curled up into a ball and kissed her knees again. I didn't go to her and I didn't ask her if she wanted to come with us. I wish now that I had, but at the time the anger in me was churning and I wanted to be away from her again.

~

Sneaky Dee's was heaving, and so full of heat I had to wipe the sweat off my upper lip as soon as we had pushed our way in. Robin and Steph were completely possessed by then, in a way that made me feel invisible, which was fine. It was enough that I'd cried in front of both of them and let them see how weird things were between me and Hetty.

The music was familiar but I couldn't find the tune and then I couldn't see Robin or Steph and there seemed to be big, wide men all around me, so wet with sweat it was spraying off them as they moved. It hadn't been a good idea to come. I was tired and heavy from seeing Hetty even though it meant she was safe, and I couldn't bear Steph and Robin seeing any more of my vulnerability.

I let myself move slowly towards the stairs, trying not to push at anyone on my way, despite seeing the lights in people's eyes that covered their pupils and meant they wouldn't have noticed someone trying to make them move anyway. The door to the street was heavy and I pushed at it until a bouncer opened it for me from the other side, smiling with his cheeks at me.

It was brisk outside, and I breathed the night in deep. I'd go home and lie with Hetty. She would be sad that I'd left her at home and hadn't wanted to talk to her. I still didn't want to, but maybe we could listen to some music and fall asleep together.

I wondered how Faith was, what she was doing, as I walked towards Marjorie. I missed her cool fingers. I hoped she knew that I was in love with her. I knew then that I was and even though it hurt it also felt huge, like a sunflower in bloom. Maybe I'd text her in the morning. That way, she wouldn't have to answer me.

All the lights were off when I got back to the house. I could smell the mulled wine still sitting, no longer warm, on the stove. Whitney came to say hello as I stood in the bathroom, cleaning my face with one of Hetty's baby wipes, the ones she used to take off her mascara that made her smell like powder. I brushed my teeth slowly, watching my cheeks move a little as I edged the toothbrush back and forth, back and forth. Hetty was terrible at brushing her teeth—would say she hated it, it was boring, she couldn't bear to do it. Would drag herself to the bathroom once every couple of nights to do a half-hearted job. Despite this, her teeth were royal, white, clean. Mine were crooked and slightly stained—too big for my mouth.

I could see the lump of Hetty in the bed when I opened our bedroom door. She shifted, whimpered and put her hand up to shield her face from the light.

'Sorry, Het.'

'It's okay,' her sleep voice said.

BRACKISH
where the two waters meet

The next morning, early, I woke up and saw that Hetty wasn't beside me. I was puffy in my fingers and eyelids and feet, as if the night before had flooded inside me and needed to be wrung out. There weren't any messages from Faith, and even though I hadn't let myself wish before I checked my phone, I had hoped anyway that she might have reached out during the dark, perhaps missing me.

I could hear the faint echo of voices downstairs, and perhaps the flight of Hetty's, and lifted myself up to go down and see how she was. Light streamed in through the window where the curtain hadn't been pulled across completely. It was bright on different parts of me as I walked around trying to find something to pull over my legs.

Whitney met me on the stairs and we padded down to the kitchen together. The radio was on, and Dill and Hetty were sitting at the table, eating toast and nearing the end of laughter that seemed relaxed, happy. Dill smiled at me, patted the seat next to him. 'Nessy. How did you sleep?'

'Good, thank you.'

Hetty looked up from spreading peanut butter on her slice and smiled at me. She looked very tired, her eyes lidded and her lips bruised. I wanted to go over and cuddle her and tell her everything would be absolutely fine and that she could lean on me, but I knew that couldn't be true, at least the everything-would-be-fine part. I sat down and let Dill pour me a coffee from the drip jug. Hetty went to the fridge and got the milk, pouring just enough into my cup.

'Hetty's been telling me that she's looking for a new job,' Dill said, presumably trying to get Hetty and me to talk to each other.

I was shy behind my sheet of half-asleep. Hetty was inspecting her breakfast as if she had never eaten peanut butter and didn't know what toast was. The kitchen sat still around us.

'Yeah, Het?' I asked.

She looked up at me again, this time with no smile.

'Yeah.'

Her voice sounded a bit thick, like she had a sore throat or a blocked nose. I wondered if she had finally realised Elaine was mean and not much else, or whether she'd been fired after missing a shift and calls and everything.

'How come?'

She didn't answer. Just sat there, eyes back on her toast.

Dill put his hand on her arm and lowered his voice this time when he spoke, almost cooing. 'Tell her.'

I heard a small sigh come from her mouth and saw her shoulders rise and then drop beneath her thin dressing gown.

I loved that gown. It was made of bright-pink polyester, fuchsia perhaps, and had a round, decadent collar darted with yellow cotton flowers. Hetty had found it in an op shop in Croydon when we were younger and used to drive out there in my mum's car on Saturdays to buy lots of things we would never wear. She had held that pink up against her and asked me whether she should buy it, shaking her head as if she didn't want to hear me. I had whooped yes and pulled it from her to wrap around myself. It smelt like potpourri, no matter how many times she washed it, and had no lining.

She looked hard at me now.

'Elaine died. She died, and Ronnie's won't be the same without her.'

Her mouth was round for the 'on' in 'Ronnie's' and 'without'. It sounded like she was singing me a strange song.

I didn't understand. Elaine had died? I looked at Dill, who was looking at me with a face that was worried, that had probably been worried in that way since he had started having breakfast with Hetty. His eyebrows told me now that he was confused.

Hetty didn't elaborate. I noticed her fingers picking at the edge of her piece of toast. The peanut butter had melted and was thickening again and she hadn't had a bite yet.

'Elaine died? Oh, Hetty. How did she die? That's so awful.'

'Yes. It is awful,' Dill said, raising his eyebrows at me.

Hetty didn't look up or answer again. The worry grew in my stomach.

'Het? What happened?'

She looked at me harder and clicked her tongue. 'How

would I know? I wouldn't know. No one will *tell* me!'

The worry spun now, up my arms, down my legs, around and around in my stomach. Her voice was still thick, and it seemed more like a thickness in her head now, that had filled up her throat and her nose too: that was suffocating her.

'What do you mean? I don't—'

'I got to work and they said she was dead. That's it. I can't go back there. It's diseased. I felt like it was diseased and now I know it is.'

'But you love it there, Het. You love working there.'

'Elaine's gone,' she said, and now there were tears rolling fast from her eyes. 'She's gone.'

Dill and I looked at each other, and Hetty cried and held her face with her hands, and I saw the tears running through the gaps between her fingers and imagined how warm they must be. The peanut butter spread so carefully against her toast had congealed. My heart hurt desperately for her and I was starting to feel sick again, though I didn't yet understand what was happening.

We sat with Hetty until she stopped crying. She told us she was going to get dressed and go out to find another job.

'I think I'd like to work in the Eaton Centre,' she said with her hands on her hips after getting up from the table. 'It's magical there.'

Hetty hated shopping centres.

'I went swimming there the other day, Ness, did you know that?'

I shook my head. There were no swimming pools at the Eaton Centre, unless she meant in the hotel that sat at the top of it. She couldn't afford to swim there. I looked at Dill but he was furrowed and watching Hetty like she might explode.

'I didn't know there was a pool there?' I said.

Hetty didn't hear me or didn't want to answer me, and picked up her peanut-butter plate. She started to whistle as she moved towards the bin and put the toast in; then she left the kitchen.

'What the hell is going on?' Dill moved his hand through his hair, worrying the strands. 'She's not making sense.'

'I know...I don't know.'

Dill was still pulling his hand through his hair, his other one tapping the table. 'I mean—her boss isn't dead, is she? And even if she is, it's not because Ronnie's is diseased? And talking about going swimming at the Eaton Centre is just—'

He stopped and stood up, walking to the sink, where a window looked out onto the street.

'There just aren't any swimming pools at the Eaton Centre.'

I nodded. It was scary to have seen Hetty like that, all gently wired and full of sadness and plummeting towards complete nonsense. I didn't want her going out with peanut-butter fingers to walk magically around the Eaton Centre talking about swimming pools and her dead boss, and asking people for a job.

I told Dill I didn't know what was happening but I would try to sort it out, and went upstairs to talk to Hetty.

She was busying herself in our bedroom, talking to Whitney as she picked out something to wear. On the bed lay three of her dresses—butter blue, red wine, teal. I sat down among them, picking up the blue one to smooth its crinkled collar.

Hetty didn't iron things; she had never needed to. Her face suited the extra creases. I took a deep breath into the bottom of my belly. I needed to try to tell her that she wasn't making sense, to see if she could try to.

'Het, can you sit down a minute?'

She was over at the chest of drawers scrambling through jewellery. All hers—I didn't own anything other than a pine-cone brooch my mother had given me when I turned twenty-one and a best-friend broken-heart charm from Hetty. I was wearing the charm, and brought my hand up to finger it. I loved to feel along the jagged edge where the heart had been broken in two. Jagged but smooth, like our friendship. Hetty's half said *Best* and mine said *Friend*. It had always seemed appropriate.

'Ness, can we talk later? I need to get going.'

'Where are you off to?' I wanted to hear her say something different, something less strange.

'I told you! The Eaton Centre.'

'But Het, you don't want to work there, do you, really? You hate how they have no windows, and the trays everyone eats their meals off in the food court.'

We had sometimes visited Eastland Shopping Centre in Ringwood when we were younger and boredom got the better of us. It was a basic, unworldly sort of a place—Hetty couldn't stand it. I liked to feel the cool of the artificial air and walk slowly around not really looking inside any of the shops, buying cinnamon donuts and eating them from their pink bag, wiping my sugar fingers and letting the crystals fall free onto the shiny floor, but Hetty became unruly in there. She seemed to claw at the air, and she pulled at where her clothing met her neck. She hated everyone—other shoppers, sales staff, the guards out the front. Hetty didn't usually hate people, especially not straight away. I remembered she had said she would die if she ever got locked in there.

'Yes, I do,' she said shortly, as if she didn't have time for such questions. As if her truth was waiting. My heart was still rapid; something was still wrong.

'Hetty—I have to go to work today, But I can come with you to the Eaton Centre tomorrow?'

She sighed heavily, picking her floppy bag up off the floor.

'You could just rest today? You seem so tired...'

She looked at me coldly. Her eyes were mostly white, as if I was someone she barely knew, didn't know at all.

'I'm not tired. I don't need to rest. The early bird gets the worm,' she added, with none of the light irony I would expect, no curving up of her lips to make a smile. Her face was long and smooth, with no lightness or lines.

I let her past, noticing that she had blushed her cheeks so much it looked like she'd been burnt across her cheekbones, like she was about to turn into a clown.

A strong scent of alcohol—bourbon, maybe, with that hot, sweet smell it had—lingered in the room after I had heard her clomp down the stairs and slam the front door. She hadn't said goodbye to Dill, who was still in the kitchen, and who she loved. I knew she loved him, but this wasn't Hetty.

I needed to figure out what to do to bring her back. I wasn't upset that she seemed to hate me all of a sudden, though it hurt to have her gone like that. I just felt like I needed to keep her out of the world until she was herself again. It was as if she had been worked on in the night and put back together wrong. If she was out there among strangers too long, something bad would happen. I could feel it.

I was late for work and texted Minnie to tell her as I left the house. *This is fine, take your time x* she replied quickly, so I let myself move lightly as I walked down our street. I would tell Minnie about how Hetty had been and see what she thought. She was calm, and erred on the side of caution, clarity, taking the time something needed before coaxing it out or making a decision about it. She cooked like that, worked like that. I could see the pleasure she gave our few customers with her grace. I imagined she would have sex like that, would kiss like that—carefully, without even the notion of bodily violence.

Then I remembered Faith and looked down at my phone, imagining how happy I would be if there was a sudden text there from her telling me she missed me, or asking me to see her again soon. There was nothing.

~

My walk to work had changed over the past few weeks, in the green and pink of the flowers and grass and leaves of the trees. It was a red, brown, yellow walk that crunched, and I felt like autumn was what I had needed. The air no longer had that tired drench to it and the faces of those I passed appeared drier, more contained, less flushed with heat.

I took a photo of the same tree every time I walked this route: a young horse chestnut near the part of Beverley Street where the park became the art gallery. It had been slim and leafless the first time I saw it, back when I started at Cafe Art Song and had just moved into Marjorie. Five months later it had a full head of leaves, and they were now blushing, curling, almost ready to fall.

    I hadn't shown Hetty any of these photos, though I was proud of them, proud that I had chosen to concentrate the lens of my phone on such unpredictable, quiet beauty. Faith had loved them when I showed her, flicking through the photos with my thumb on her bed one night. She had told me I was an artist and only laughed a bit before putting her fingers inside me one by one until I was up against the bedhead, gasping.

    It felt stupid to take the photo today but I did anyway, in the hope that things would be back to happy, to normal again soon. As always I took it quickly, not wanting those walking by to notice me and think something of me. The leaves were swaying that day in the wind.

    By the time I had reached the corner opposite the gallery, a block from work, I wondered if it would be okay to call Hetty to see where and how she was. I stopped myself from putting my hand into my pocket for my phone and stood there counting the amount of seconds it took to fill my body up with air, and how many to empty it.

    There wasn't any point calling her now. She would be at the Eaton Centre wandering around, being surreal. Why would things have changed in the hour since I had seen her, stormy and yet so clear about her mission, leaving Marjorie with a plan she would bash down anyone to see through? I wondered what the sales assistants were thinking as she entered their shops thrusting her résumé at them, not in the mood for small talk, not even in the mood for being herself: Hetty, so charming and employable. She could look wild and mean when she didn't smile, which I'd always appreciated. I imagined her at her wildest and meanest, over there in the climate-controlled mecca of the Eaton, putting off the perfectly put-together.

Minnie was sitting out the front of the cafe and seemed to have been waiting for me. Her black hair was pulled back with a soft black bow, and she was tapping at a calculator and pencilling numbers in a notebook. She looked up and gave me that smile, so disarmed and gentle.

'How are you, Ness?' She picked up a small napkin and dabbed one side of her mouth, watching me. I saw that there were a few small bowls beside her work, filled with fringed vegetables, tiny crisp fish and sprouts.

'I'm okay.'

'Sit,' she said, and pulled out the chair beside her.

'Oh, I better go in and get ready to start my shift,' I said, hoping she might insist that I didn't do that just yet.

I wanted to tell her about how Hetty had been that morning and share my worry with her. The day seemed long ahead of me while Hetty was anywhere doing anything in the same body with what seemed like a different mind. I wanted to pick her up and take her back to Marjorie, lock her in our bedroom until I could work out what to do. Minnie would at least empathise, hold some of the weight for me through this day.

The phone rang from inside the cafe. Minnie placed her hand on my shoulder.

'I'll be back soon. Eat some of this, will you?' She pointed at the tiny bowls.

I could see the glisten of sesame oil on some of them. I loved sesame oil. Beneath the sick of Hetty, my tummy growled and then the nausea became a wave that rolled over the small hunger, crashing it down and away.

I watched Minnie through the window and placed a small slither of zucchini in my mouth with my fingers. She was on the cordless and was pacing, just slightly. Then she looked out at me, took the phone from her ear and pressed at it with her finger.

'Sorry, Ness,' she said after she had sat down next to me, the floppy bow slightly lower in her hair from the interruption. She placed her hands in her lap and look out across the street.

'Are you okay, Min?'

She didn't answer for a few breaths and then pulled her eyes away from the road to me. 'Yes, sorry. Yes,' she said loudly. 'Have you eaten?'

Minnie and food.

'I'm fine, Min. Thank you, though.'

She smiled. 'You seem tired, Ness. Anything wrong?' She smoothed her hair with the fingers of one small hand, and watched me. 'How is Hetty?'

It was becoming obvious that I wouldn't just be able to work a normal day and smile and laugh and sneak pieces of roasted seaweed or cheese when the customers weren't looking like I usually did, knowing Hetty was out there, lofty and unaware.

'She's not good.'

I told Minnie about Hetty announcing that Elaine had died and that she wanted to work at the Eaton Centre. Minnie was confused, and even paused to try to remember whether in fact there was a swimming pool at the Eaton Centre, which we agreed was an impossibility—a sort of wonderful untruth—and a sign that Hetty was unravelling.

'It wasn't even really the content of what she was saying, though I know it's weird to say that you've been swimming at the Eaton Centre,' I said, picking at one of my nails with another one, hoping the bit would come off without pain. 'It was the way she was talking, and her eyes. They were wild, Min. It sounds weird, but they were wild.'

'It doesn't sound weird. It sounds like she's really unwell.'

Hearing it from Minnie hurt. She was a thoughtful person who wouldn't make drama where there wasn't some already.

'I don't think she has any idea what's happening to her. I mean, neither do I, but it's like she has no idea what she's doing, or how different she's being. It's scaring me, and usually I'd tell her about it but I can't just—'

I stopped. Talking about it was making it worse. Nothing bad had happened, not really.

Minnie was nodding. 'I know, Ness. I know.'

'What should I do?'

'Has she ever been like this before?'

I shook my head, then thought about it. Hetty had been like this before, actually. She had been like this for splotches of time ever since I had known her, though never so boldly, or with such apparent disdain for her own safety, her own wellbeing.

I remembered the holiday we had taken the year after we finished high school, to Fraser Island, and how Hetty had climbed out of the tent early one morning to 'see the volcano'. There was no volcano, she had whispered when she got back, hours later and burnt red, and she was confused about why she had thought there was.

I remembered when Sean died and Hetty had told me she was Mary Magdalene after drinking half a bottle of vodka in the park near her family's house in Heathmont—late summer, no shoes, her cheeks glowing from the evening sun. I had thought it was grief and pain, but maybe it was more about her brain slowly changing.

My phone moved in my pocket and I heard the ring.

Minnie moved her eyes and nodded.

I didn't recognise the number, but that wasn't unusual. I only had a few numbers saved in my second-hand Blackberry. I hoped it was Hetty, somehow, and that she was herself.

'Hello?'

'Ness?'

'Yes?'

'It's Elaine.'

So she was still alive, not gone like Hetty believed. I could see her leaning against the bar, those fierce scars licking the insides of her pale arms, her short hair scraped back. She suited the practicality of managing a beer barn—lifting and tossing and pushing people out the door. Telling them no when they'd had too much and wanted more.

'Hi.'

'Look, I'm calling about Hetty. She's quit and something's not right with her—I don't think it has been for a while, actually, and I guess you're the one who might be able to help, or—'

She stopped, and I could hear the small din of music in her background. Ronnie's wouldn't be open yet, but she was definitely there, getting ready for another night of pulling ale into glasses in that cave.

I waited. I wasn't going to fill up her silence. I was sick of helping other people find their words.

'I think she's really lost it.'

I nodded, but didn't make a sound. I wasn't scared of Elaine now. I realised she might have been watching Hetty all along.

'Are you there?'

I could heard the flint in her voice.

'Yep, I'm here,' I said.

'I wonder if you've thought about helping her to go see someone? Like a psychiatrist? My sister saw one through the government program and it can be helpful, I guess.'

I waited, hearing the push and pull of her breath through the speaker before I replied. 'I think that's a good idea.'

'So you're worried too?'

It was strange to hear Elaine say the word *worried*. I flinched briefly at her solemnity. It was scary how far Hetty had let herself spill. This confirmed it.

'Yep, I am. Leave it with me.'

I hung up the phone, not waiting for Elaine's voice again. Things seemed sped up and slightly slowed down, and I didn't feel like I had time to care about goodbyes and thank-yous.

I told Minnie I had to go. If Elaine was worried and I was worried and Dill was worried, then I needed to try to find Hetty and work something out. Minnie bundled me out the door with a salted-chocolate macaron wrapped in tissue paper.

Walking quickly across and down towards the Eaton Centre, I remembered something I'd wanted to ask Elaine for quite a while. I pressed the green phone button on the last number and waited.

'Ness.'

'Yeah, hey.'

I felt like I was getting to know Elaine pretty quickly, something I had never wanted or imagined. But she was reliable, and easy to communicate with, in a way. She didn't mind me just saying whatever it was I needed to say, and that was helpful.

'What's Hetty been using?'

There was a pause, and I couldn't hear her breath this time, or any music. I wondered if she'd cut out.

'Like, drugs?' she finally asked.

'Yeah.'

'Well, I don't know everything. A bit of speed, I think. And she keeps buying mushrooms from my friend Tom. And she was high at work a few weeks ago, I think from them. Bit my arm and told a customer to stop reading her mind.'

I felt anger yell inside me.

'Why didn't you tell someone? Tell me? That's crazy!'

I hadn't known Hetty had been behaving erratically all over the place. I hadn't known she was buying mushrooms over and over and using them before work. I hoped I would have done something if I had. I was sure I would have tried.

'Yeah, I know. But she was normal the next day. The same old Hetty. And she was embarrassed when I told her, couldn't remember it. Said she did that when she was tired, and that she had a really low threshold for hallucinogens.'

I scoffed.

'I don't know what I would have done, even if I had done

something. But I'm sorry I didn't let you know. She loves you. She tells me you're her guardian angel.'

There was an ache at the end of Elaine's voice and I felt it land in me. I was Hetty's guardian, the way she had once been mine. I felt my eyes become wet and swallowed the crying down so Elaine wouldn't hear it. I didn't want to see how far this tender part of her could go.

'It's okay,' I said. 'I know it's not easy. She's not easy.'

We both said nothing for a while, then let each other go. Elaine asked if I could keep her updated and I agreed, asking the same of her in return. In that moment I felt like we understood each other, at least in relation to Hetty, and it felt right to type her name next to her number in my phone and press Save.

POOL
a quiet place in a stream

It was cold in the Eaton Centre. I called Hetty after I'd walked through the revolving door, past three different women sitting with containers for money in front of them, their faces towards the ground. I dropped a loonie in each of their cups, trying not to seem condescending as I did it. There were so many people desperately needing help in this city, I thought, as I stood there next to them, listening to the sound of my phone calling Hetty's.

There was no answer. I didn't leave a message, didn't feel like there was a point. Hetty was a dandelion of energy and fever dreams, and she wouldn't be checking her voicemail.

I walked towards the lowest level, where the food court was. Down an escalator, then some stairs, then another escalator. Maybe I could sit and think up a plan before I started my search of the shops above. It was noisy and messy in the food court. People sat at square tables with rectangular trays in front of them. They seemed to be talking and eating at the same time, having conversations I would never hear. I could smell fried-chicken batter—all-spice, stale oil—and boiled hot dogs. I still wasn't hungry.

Hetty loomed in front of me just as I finally found a table with a chair waiting, one not filled by a warm, strange body. My insides yelped, as if this was actually the greatest shock so far.

'Ness!'

She seemed to be puffing slightly, and had two round red circles for cheeks. Hetty's face didn't redden the way mine did—her nose didn't swell and glow, just stayed small and pale, leaving only her cheeks to pretty with the colour. She looked gorgeous.

'Ness, I'm so glad I bumped into you!'

She pulled at my arm, dragging me towards a salad-bar counter. There was no acknowledgment that it was remarkable that we had in fact bumped into each other, or that either of us was there at all.

'I've just ordered something. I haven't eaten in a while.' A laugh showed in her neck, stretched and rippling.

I heard her name called out from behind us and turned to see a woman waiting behind the counter with a tray. Hetty didn't seem to hear.

'Het, is that yours?' I asked her.

She spun around, hair flying. 'Oh, yes! Yes!'

We sat at a table that still held the trays of its previous tenants, abandoned. There was an empty McDonald's chip box and a half-eaten sandwich. I could see the edge of some ham at one end of it, pink and curled like a tongue. Hetty shovelled salad into her mouth, the dressing leaving an oil slick on her lips.

Now that I had found her, and so soon, I didn't know what to say. I felt as if it wouldn't really matter if I was completely honest and told her I was worried she was ill, and that I thought she needed to stop her life and her bizarre plans and seek help. She wouldn't be affected by it, because she wasn't really there. I wondered where the real Hetty had gone—was she still there, just below the surface, or was her soul resting somewhere else, waiting?

'I'm really worried about you, Hetty,' I said carefully, wanting to make ground while I had her in front of me, before she flew away again.

She kept shovelling, then wiped her mouth with the back of an elegant hand.

'Have you been feeling unwell lately? Tell me what's happening. You seem very different.'

It was strange to admit to her that she wasn't herself. It could be the catalyst for her to explode, or to pull off her face like it was a mask and reveal the face of La Ciguapa or a banshee, predicting her own death and leading others towards theirs—as if our lives were a horror movie and this a scene near the end.

Hetty looked up at me from her plastic plate and swallowed. 'I'm just feeling good. Different in a good way. Well, mostly good. I think I've decided who I want to be, and it's tiring, but that's the way it should be, shouldn't it?'

She hadn't quite finished the mouthful of food she had taken before I asked my questions, and as she talked I could see bits of corn and the white green of baby-cos leaves in her mouth, opening and closing. I wanted to look away. Hetty didn't eat with her mouth open.

'There's nothing wrong. You don't need to be *threatened*,' she spat.

Threatened. She thought I was jealous of her, jealous of this jangled energy that was spinning her out into oblivion. Jealous of her chaos and her fake friends and the delusion she had draped all over herself.

'I'm not threatened! Jesus. You have no idea what's actually going on anymore.'

The comment bounced off her and she resumed shovelling the salad, holding her hair back with one hand, barely chewing.

'Hetty. I think you need to see a doctor. I can't help you, and you need help.'

This time she didn't look up. I watched her jaw move up and down, and her throat get big like there was an animal in there and then not big as she swallowed the vegetables down. She finished and kept her face towards her plate.

'I'm not going to bother explaining it to you.' Her voice was low, each word sounded out as though I was stupid. 'I've been lucky enough to be given this chance. I've heard things you wouldn't dream of. Don't take this away from me.'

I shivered all the way from my neck to the bottom of my spine. I didn't want to bring her to me and cuddle her anymore, tell her it would be okay. I wanted to get away from her, and she wanted that too. Tears welled in my eyes as I watched her stand.

'You'll understand soon,' she said to the side of my face, as if I was gone now and she was talking to a faint idea of me. Then she turned and walked away, and I started to cry. The tears were only thin, and I didn't make any noise as I let them come out and gulped and choked a little. My body was too tired to give the act of sorrow anything more.

~

I cried those thin, quiet tears all afternoon and all night, though nobody seemed to notice. Hetty didn't come home for dinner and she wasn't back by midnight. I swatted the buzz of worry away and didn't move or look at my phone. From our bed I watched the sky out the window, blue-black and familiar like any night sky in any country.

I tried to remember other times when Hetty had been mad, even just almost-mad. I knew it wasn't the right word but I couldn't figure out how else to think about her, with those eyes. She wouldn't go and see a doctor, ask for a diagnosis. She probably thought I needed one.

I wished again that we were stronger people, she and I. That we had built up a level of fight within us and within our relationship that I could lean on. Instead, Hetty told me to leave her alone and I simply did. It was pathetic.

I lay in my softest T-shirt and thought about the months before we had flown to Toronto, sifting through the memories. Hetty had still been grieving Sean, despite the muck that covered everything they had shared and everything about him.

A few months before we set off, she had told me she wanted to bury the letter he'd left for her—a suicide note that had blamed her for his death—and that she was sure this would help with the pain and the guilt and the mire he had left on her vision of everything.

We drove one misty morning to the park that edged the

Yarra River in Fairfield and walked through a section that wasn't really meant for walking, dense with the low branches of yellow gums and ironbarks, riparian shrubs and shoots of feather-spear grass. Hetty was soundless in a different way to her normal quiet: as though she had forgotten I was there. She stopped with certainty at a spot that looked just like every other spot, and asked that we stop there. I sat and she kneeled to dig up a small bit of earth, telling me this was the place she had imagined, and that the pain might be able to rest here.

I understood then what she was doing, or I thought I understood. I couldn't access her grief for the loss of Sean, but I believed in it and wanted it gone. We took the dried bits of plant she had chosen—rosemary, lemon balm and sage—from their plastic bag and placed them in the small candle lamp she had brought. She asked me to fold up Sean's letter and I did so carefully, even though I wanted to rip it up and scream at her to let him go in the same way he had let her go—as if she didn't matter, as if he wanted her to suffer forever. She was crying when I handed her the small folded bit of notepaper, grubby from all our fingerprints. We had decided together what she would say that morning, and now she said it carefully. No apology. I couldn't let her say sorry to him.

'Goodbye, Sean. That's all now. I can't give you anything else. I really do hope you rest in peace.'

Then we lit the letter and the sticks and leaves with a lighter, and watched the bundle flame and smoke and become crisp and then nothing, and Hetty buried all of it in the sticky soil, and we sat.

It got cold we sat there so long, even though it was January and the sun was high until late. Hetty suggested we go get drunk, and leaving the car behind we walked all the way to Collingwood in the dusk, and drank beer out of sweaty jugs at the Grace Darling. She did drink heavily that night, and she told me all sorts of things Sean had done to her over the years, things that made me press my nails into my palms so hard that blood appeared.

    I lay on the bed in Toronto and wondered how she had been well for so long, with such a monster hanging over her. It was no wonder things were unravelling.

MEANDER
the river flows in sweeping meanders

After four days I realised that this time no one knew where Hetty was—not Rick, not Elaine, not anyone who lived at Marjorie with us, not me. We had a house dinner and Dill cooked and no one ate very much, and we talked about what Hetty had been like lately and what we could do when she came back again, and it felt a little bit okay for a while and then bad again after everyone went on with their nights and I was alone at the kitchen table with Whitney below me. She seemed to know something was wrong and kept kissing my legs with her tiny mouth, but I didn't feel better because of it; I felt as if I was useless.

I could hear the muffled bawl of the wind outside and wondered if Hetty was ploughing through it to somewhere or if she was safe and warm. I was beginning to understand what the winter would be like—short of breath, desolate, washed out. The fall was lush and invigorating, but it was coming to an end.

The next morning Hetty still wasn't beside me, and when I texted Elaine her reply was the same as it had been for days: *No word here.* I put the phone down and heaved myself up to dress for work, deciding what to wear through the murk in my head. It rang as I scuffled through my clothes drawer and my heart lifted—if it was Hetty I would love her and thank her and help her come home with my kindness. I promised myself this as I went to answer it.

It was Faith. I heard my voice when I said hello, soft and not a question, just a statement. I heard Faith reply the same way.

I had missed her, and told her with my insides stammering. She told me she'd missed me too. She asked me how I was and I told her I would tell her when I saw her and then I asked if I could see her and she said of course.

We agreed to meet that afternoon in the place that I thought of as the mini-amphitheatre, to the side of the Ontario College of Art and Design building, where older people in bright loose outfits did tai chi in the mornings and later students sat smoking after class. It had sloped edges and what could be a stage at the centre. It was near Cafe Art Song, and Faith was planning to spend the day taking photographs of people outside the small, old-fashioned mall across the road.

When I arrived at work my mind was full of Faith and Hetty, and I was glad we were busy. There were a few groups of students from a high school nearby who had spent the morning at the art gallery and needed lunch, and they stayed for almost two hours: one harried teacher and fifteen young people. Then we had a few small groups of older couples who wanted coffee and cake, and the rest of the day passed quickly.

After I'd finished my shift, I saw there was no word from Hetty but Elaine had tried to call me. I knew I should call her back, that if she was calling and not texting there must be news, but I wanted to hold out and see Faith first. It was busy on Dundas Street and the sky was yellow where it wasn't grey-blue. I loved it like that.

I saw Faith waiting at the edge of the mini-amphitheatre before she saw me. She was sitting and watching a mother and child playing near her, and she was smiling. Faith didn't scroll through her phone when she was out in the world. She liked to take in what was happening around her. I had noticed this and told her I knew it about her. She had been surprised, and genuinely interested to know that this was rare. Most of the people my age I saw around Toronto and Melbourne had their eyes turned down and their hand holding their phones so they could see the screens, despite the glare of the sun they weren't acknowledging, or the beginning of the dusk they wouldn't witness. Faith wasn't like other people.

Before I got to her she looked over and saw me. She smiled even more and I could see she really was glad. I felt sick with relief.

'Ness,' she said when I had joined her and we were hugging. She breathed it into my hair and my ear, and it was so instantly mollifying I realised just how much I had needed her these past few weeks.

'Oh,' was all I could say for a while, and we stayed close together until I wondered if I was suffocating her and moved away.

She looked excited: flushed cheeks and wisps of hair blowing up against her face. It felt wonderful to be near her again after time apart, and I hoped I didn't look too tired or dirty. I smiled too, letting the breeze that circled us do its dance. It was important to just be there with Faith, and I tried to let go of my worry about Hetty.

'How are you?' Faith asked me, her eyes searching.

'I'm good. I missed you. I'm okay. But how are you?'

I wanted to say nothing or not very much and just have our eyes looking at each other, but too many words stumbled out. It was so strange to see her after all the thoughts I'd had about her since last time. She seemed hyper-real somehow, and my palms were lightly sweating.

Before she could answer I spoke again. 'I like your coat.'

She was wearing a loose dark-red trench coat made of a soft, brushed fabric. It made her look even smaller than she usually did, as if she was hiding. I wanted to rub the material against my cheek, my neck.

'Thank you,' she said, pulling at the two parts of the collar, bringing it in towards her clavicle. 'It's from the Leslieville Value Village.'

'Ah. Because no one but you would understand this red,' I said, and pulled her to me again to kiss her forehead. I felt shy around her despite how brief the break between us had been, and I wanted to touch her and kiss her somewhere dim and private.

I pulled away from her and looked at her face, still pink, still shining. 'Can we go back to yours?'

She shook her head quickly, firmly, and I felt everything inside me drop. I shouldn't have asked. It was too much. She had never planned to sleep with me again, just wanted to make sure I was okay—to be friends, or something horrific like that.

I heard her sigh slightly. 'Not today,' she said. Her eyes were sad.

'Of course, of course—sorry. I shouldn't have said that.'

'No. It's okay. I just can't yet.'

'Of course. You don't have to explain—'

She took me by my shoulders with her small hands, lightly. 'I want to, Ness. But I need to know that I can without feeling anxious again.'

'Anxious?'

I waited and watched her but she didn't say anything. She was looking at her hands now, and I didn't want to disturb her.

Around us, people sat or stood against the circle of the amphitheatre. The mother and child had left. There were students a little way around. Two girls, both wearing thick-heeled boots, both smoking long thin cigarettes. I could smell clove in the air.

Finally, Faith looked up at me again. 'Anxious about Hetty.'

She looked so worried, standing there. I felt a wave of something roll through my body, almost like nostalgia. Hetty. Faith's idea of Hetty, as a beautiful tall creature dripping with other people's tears. Swimming the length of a pool filled with blood in a bikini. I wished she knew Hetty the way I did. Knew the pool was actually full of rainwater. She would one day, if I could just behave myself.

'Oh, Faith. Please don't be anxious about Hetty—'

She was shaking her head and looking at her hands again. I needed to stop saying Hetty's name. This wasn't about her—or maybe it was, but I wanted that part to be over.

'I understand, though. I do,' I said.

She looked up and smiled.

'Will we stake out the Korean supermarket for Margaret, then?'

She nodded and laughed, a peal against the dusk that had arrived around us. I took her hand and we turned and started up towards Bloor Street. The sky was pink now, edged with purple.

~

On Bloor we took a streetcar along to Koreatown. The supermarket was lit up against the dark of the sky, and we walked inside and took a basket each so we could move through the aisles and wait for her without looking like we weren't planning to buy anything.

I chose a box of biscuit sticks tipped with pink frosting, the front depicting a panda with a smile and a strawberry hat, and gave it to Faith. She solemnly placed it in her basket and nodded, making us both laugh. No one noticed us; the supermarket was big enough. There was a delicate, tinkly song playing on the speakers and the air was crisp.

I was happy to be there, physically and mentally separate from my worries about Hetty. There, under the fluorescent lighting, with tiny Faith in her soft coat, I felt happy and silly. We wouldn't see Margaret Atwood, because those kinds of things didn't happen to me, and what would she be buying at this time of the night? I imagined she would have had an early dinner of vegetables and legumes, and would now be writing at her desk, a sprawling mahogany one, maybe with a view of a tree, maybe with a cup of something. No one seemed to shop at this hour, aside from older men who had forgotten to eat. I watched one shuffle past us, his sandals barely lifting off the linoleum floor for each step.

In the noodle aisle we kissed, and Faith moved her hand under my jumper and then my T-shirt to find my stomach skin. I still felt like I became a glow-worm when she touched me. It was delicious and overwhelming, and I wanted to ask if we could go outside and stand beside a shopfront in the dark so we could kiss more and touch more away from the gleam.

I didn't say anything. I could feel Faith's body poised to jump away from me if I pushed too hard. She was springy in her shoulders and her eyes were bright.

In my basket I had white kimchi and a box of tissues decorated with a watercolour painting of a river edged with trees. Faith had the strawberry sticks and three grape sodas—for her family, she said, who liked to sip at them when Faith visited and they watched home videos together. I told her that my family had never made any home videos, and she told me I was lucky. I told her I wondered what it might be like to see yourself as a child, moving and talking and playing. Faith said it wasn't all that special; that it was dissociative, and that's why her parents loved it.

We'd been wandering the aisles for half an hour, and even the man stocking the shelves who had seemed almost asleep was watching us now. We needed to give up and leave, but I didn't want to be the one to suggest it.

Faith looked up at me from where we stood in front of the

frozen shrimp. 'I guess we should go?'

I nodded, and took her hand to hold it carefully. She seemed disappointed, though I had been sure we'd both expected nothing. She had an optimism that was unruly, Faith. It wandered out in front of her and tripped her up sometimes.

'I hope one day I see her,' Faith said quietly as we walked towards the front of the store where we would pay for our pink sticks and our purple bubbles, and our white kimchi streaked with red.

There was a woman in line for the cash register. She had on a purple-and-green woollen hat—a toque, not a beanie, I reminded myself—and a long scarf of the same yarn that she had wrapped around herself. It wasn't so cold that night, and I wondered why she was bundled as if it was icy or stormy.

There was nowhere to put our things yet—the woman was buying a large amount of kimchi and blood-red gochujang paste, and she had set them up in two neat rows that filled the length of the conveyer belt. The man who had been shelving was now at the cash register. I watched the delicate fingers of the woman making sure each tall tub of kimchi didn't fall as the conveyer belt trundled and the man beeped each container against the scanner. Her hands were thin and veined with blue.

I felt Faith nudge me from behind and I turned. Her eyes were big, and she pulled me slightly back with her hand.

'It's her!' she whispered into the side of me, so I could barely hear it.

'What?' I asked.

'It's *her*.'

I turned back and saw that Faith was right: it was Margaret

Atwood. I noticed now the sprigs of hair that curled up and out from under her hat. They were white and grey. She turned as if she knew we were watching her, and smiled with the whole of her face, shaped like an elf's, with a pointed, cheeky twinkle. I felt my arm hairs stand and smiled back, as broadly as I could, to show her I loved her and that Faith did too.

I wondered if Faith would say something to her, and whether she would regret it if she didn't, and smiled again as the woman who was Margaret Atwood moved one of the plastic separators to the end and placed it down behind her kimchi so that we could begin placing our items behind hers. I saw Faith move by my side and then heard her voice, higher than usual.

'I'm so sorry to bother you, but, um, are you Margaret Atwood?' she asked, with a small laugh at the end. I turned to watch her and saw she was wringing her hands.

The woman smiled that peaked smile again and nodded slowly. 'Yes, I am,' she said, and moved one hand to take Faith's.

They held on—not shaking, not moving at all, just one small hand wrapped close around another—and then let go. It was as if they knew each other faintly, or had meant to meet there and exchange something.

'I love your books. Thank you.'

Margaret Atwood nodded. 'Do you write?' she asked Faith.

Faith reddened slightly and shook her head. 'Oh, no—no—not like you. I just read!'

Margaret Atwood laughed, and moved to turn back towards the checkout, where the man was waiting for her to pay, so bored and tired now that he was leaning on his elbows.

'Reading is the important part.'

'Yes,' we answered at the same time, nodding enthusiastically, though I was not really a reader and never would be. The glow that circled Margaret Atwood's face had disappeared when she turned; we looked at each other, Faith and I, with open mouths. We watched her pay and pick up her three canvas bags full of pickled cabbage and chilli. She turned once more to face us, the man behind the counter sighing.

'Take care,' she said, and walked out. She was small in the dark of the night outside the supermarket and she turned right as we watched, towards her house in the Annex, in her pixie shoes.

'Oh my god!' Faith said, her voice loud again. 'I can't believe we saw her!'

'Was that real?' I said, and put a hand over my mouth.

~

That night we said goodbye at College and Shaw. Faith skipped there, yelling out to no one that she had just met the love of her life, Margaret Atwood, and telling me she could now die happy.

When she slowed down and snuggled into the side of me, my arm around her shoulder, she told me she didn't think I should come stay the night, but wanted to see me again soon, and asked if that was all right. We kissed briefly as a pack of teenagers in costumes walked past us shouting, and told each other we would text.

It was cold walking the rest of the way home to Marjorie on my own. I huffed my warm breath into my jacket and wondered again where Hetty was.

LAKE
lakes lie on land and are not part of the ocean

The police came like they do in the movies, and when Ingrid answered the door they asked to speak with me. I suppose Ingrid was scared, and worried for me, so she went to Dill's room and asked him to wake me up. It was after midnight, and when he came into our bedroom and gently shook my shoulder, the first thing I thought was: Where is Hetty?

It had been seven days since I'd seen her at the Eaton Centre and I'd heard nothing. I had planned to go to the police to tell them she was missing but I didn't know when I should do it, and whether it would be something I might regret when she inevitably resurfaced.

As I walked slowly down the stairs towards the front door, I tried to prepare myself for something bad but I couldn't seem to hold the possibility. My brain felt fat inside my skull, and in the corners of my eyes there were chunks of sleep so big that it almost hurt when I blinked.

I realised near the kitchen that Dill was still beside me and that he was holding my hand. Whitney was at our feet, getting in our way, making peeping sounds. Robin and Clark were in the living room—I saw their long bodies bent against the couch, and I held my breath.

There were two police officers: one woman, one man. Their faces were lit up by our front-door bulb and they weren't smiling.

The female officer asked me if I was Vanessa and I said yes. She asked me if I knew Hetty and I said yes, but the word got caught in my throat from the fear that had arrived inside. I paused, and said it again so she could hear me, hoping the two of them could give me time. That was all I knew, then. That I needed time.

Later, in our bedroom—my bedroom, just mine now—Dill told me what the officers had said, because I'd collapsed in the doorway after they said it and I needed to hear it again.

He told me that Hetty had drowned, that she had been found dead on the shore of Cherry Beach that evening by a couple on an after-dinner walk, and that her body had been waterlogged and fully clothed, her eyes shut. The police didn't know much more yet—they were trying to find out why she had been in the water.

'But I know why,' I told him.

Dill waited, watching me.

'Because she was swimming,' I said, and he nodded. 'She was trying to find the sea.'

~

In the morning I was still awake. The policewoman had told us the night before that I would need to come to the station as soon as I could, to identify Hetty's drowned body—though she hadn't said drowned; I had added that bit in my head because it was true. I don't remember where it was I went, but I walked there in the early dark and had to bang on the door to be let in when I arrived too early.

Hetty's body was under a covering like the bodies in BBC crime shows, and I remember the colour of it—a pale yellow, like a dying cat's sick—and when they lifted the sheet I saw her grey forehead and the jump of her nose and my body ripped apart and I was screaming. I had to say that it was Hetty, and I did, but then I needed to vomit and they ordered a taxi to come and get me and I was back at Marjorie before I knew it, blinking to try to get rid of the image of her face, so still and dead.

Later, Dill gave me a valium and took me to Cherry Beach in his old green Honda Civic, and we stood on the shore. Through the loud thrum in my head I thought about how it was so unfair that I'd never even been to this beach with Hetty, that we had never even talked about how sweet the name was, that we would never come here together to laugh at the lake waves and wonder at the sand. I couldn't let myself feel anything more than that unfairness, because if I did I knew I would die too, and so I let Dill cuddle in to me, and when he asked if he should call Faith I said yes in a voice that seemed separate from me and strange—like an echo.

He took my phone and left me to stand nearby, and I wondered if I was swaying as I heard him speaking, asking Faith to come, telling her softly what had happened. It made me angry, that he could share something so private with everyone, just because it was true.

When he finished the call I asked him in a loud voice, 'What the fuck am I supposed to do?' and he shook his head with tears swishing out from his eyes, wetting the sand around us.

'Is this even real sand?' I yelled. 'I never even bothered to find out for her,' my voice said, watery with tears, my nose bleeding snot.

Hetty had been sick and I hadn't helped her at all, I told him. He shook his head but I asked him to let me have that truth, and after a while he nodded and we sat on the cold tiny crumbs of rock. Then Faith was there and I drank from the bottle she gave me and closed my eyes in the circle of their arms, and the wind felt like the passionate kisses I'd never been able to give Hetty and I knew I'd never love anyone else again.

SEA
sea is sometimes confused with see

I stayed in Toronto for three more weeks after Hetty was found and then I had to leave because she was everywhere and nowhere at the same time and I couldn't imagine not feeling terrible. Marjorie was full of the same people it had been before, and they were even more caring and available after Hetty was gone, making sure I was fed each morning and night, giving me cuddles on the stairs, letting me shower first and making me coffees I couldn't drink next to untouched plates of toast and sliced, browned apple.

I couldn't speak at the beginning, because I knew I'd let Hetty down and I knew that if I said this to anyone they would tell me I was wrong, would ask me to be kind to myself, which was impossible. I let Faith call and call, my phone vibrating on the bedside table or under the doona, my head in my hands. I let her visit me and try to talk to me and I let myself say sorry, but not much more. Nothing burned in my body or curled in my groin when I thought about Faith or when she was near me.

My pelvis was numb, my breasts hardened. Even now, I still can't orgasm the way I used to. I suppose that height of passion died along with Hetty.

After a week of eating only not to faint, and getting out of bed only not to disappear into the linen completely, I reasoned that I still loved people and should still be pretending I was alive, but that just brought more of the same guilt in a different way. I began googling Hetty's symptoms before she had walked into Lake Ontario—her autopsy had come back, and I knew now for certain she had drowned and that she had been sober when she did it, and to me that left only an illness I could have seen and could have helped her get treatment for. I read website after website that, in my mind, confirmed it.

She had been grandiose and she had been deluded at the end, and it was suddenly obvious that she had been psychotic and could have been given medication that might have helped. If she hadn't been so confused, she wouldn't have walked into the water in the way I imagined over and over she must have—perhaps crying, perhaps determined, trying to find the salt of the ocean. I felt sick in my stomach about it, and found that the only way to feel a bit less sick was to dot the insides of my arms and thighs with a safety pin until there were tiny spots of blood.

I spoke to my father briefly, then my mother for longer, and told them I was okay. Nothing else seemed to be worth telling, though when I heard my mother's voice I felt the tears spring and wished her skin was against mine and I was just a baby. I asked my parents to call Hetty's after I had tried myself and the phone had rung out every time. My mother asked in her quavery voice if I would be coming home. I told her I would be.

~

I went back to work to fill the days before I left, because I hoped it might help the thunder and the utter stillness inside me. My first shift was on a Tuesday in December, and I walked to Cafe Art Song wrapped in one of Hetty's scarves and a hat and a big dark coat. The cold we had been waiting to experience had begun but I had no one to compare notes with. I could feel how harsh the wind was as I walked, and understood why the eyes of Torontonians went dead when you asked them about winter. It was already too cold, and this was the kindest winter month. I walked along Spadina and Dundas past people wearing balaclavas as if on their way to rob a bank, and it suited my dark mood.

When I arrived at Cafe Art Song it was warm inside and Minnie hugged me for a long time. When she pulled back to look at me there were tears in her eyes.

'I am so sorry, so sorry,' she said delicately, as if I was sick or elderly.

I couldn't cry anymore, so I just nodded and thanked her and touched her shoulder so she knew she'd done enough.

We worked away together through a busy lunchtime, serving side by side, moving past each other with plates of savoury pancake and beans and bowls of berries, our hips swaying like we were dancing. I was glad for the movement and the demand, and when at three there were no customers left and the CD we had been playing ended, I was devastated. We stood in the doorway of the kitchen, looking at each other.

'I keep forgetting and thinking about what I'll say to her when I see her,' I told Minnie, who started to cry then, properly, making a small sad noise along with the tears, which made me feel terrible and almost better at the same time.

'Oh, Ness,' she said.

I didn't want her mind to be whirring, trying to work out what to say that would be most helpful. Nothing was helpful, but just having her near me seemed a comfort. That was all I could expect then, and I knew it.

'It's okay, Minnie. Don't worry. I'm just wading through,' I said, making the action of swimming with my arms, as if the sadness were a body of water and I had fallen in.

'Oh,' she said.

Over the remaining hours a few more customers came in, all on their own, all wanting cake and coffee, and I wondered what losses they had needed to bear in their lives, and whether it was etched into the lines of their faces the way mine would surely be. I tried to remember how it had felt to serve people before Hetty died but I couldn't. The serving felt like nothing now, except if I really held eyes with the person. Then it felt lonely, as if I would never really know them and that was one of the problems, though I didn't really have the energy to imagine why or what or who they were.

We closed at six after the last person wandered out, and Minnie made us lime drinks with rum. Except for that first night, I hadn't wanted to drink alcohol since Hetty had died because it felt like I would slip away from her, or that the feelings would get drunk too and I would tip over the edge. I knew it was normal to want to drink enough to block out the pain but I couldn't imagine how much it would take. Sitting there with Minnie, the rum and lime was perfect down my throat and into my tummy.

We sat at the bench that looked up and out onto the street and watched the legs and torsos of people leaving work, arm in arm, so nakedly full of life.

'Is everyone just blissfully happy except me?'

'Not me,' Minnie answered, and tipped her glass to drink.

I shrugged.

'Think about how many people aren't out walking,' Minnie said in her peaceable voice. 'There are many people who haven't left their house today because they are too sad.' She paused. 'You're not alone, I promise you.'

'Hetty was alone, though, Minnie. That's what I can't—can't get over. She must have thought she was so alone, to go into the water with all her clothes on and try to swim away.'

I'd not spoken to anyone about how much it was haunting me. I replayed the image of Hetty walking into Lake Ontario, in her boots and her long dress with the velvet cuffs and her pepper-coloured corduroy jacket, over and over. She had cared about those clothes; she had cared about her life, and me, and lots of things; and yet she'd said goodbye to all of it. Two weeks after she had been found, the pathologists had made their decision—suicide. My heart and lungs burned.

'She wasn't well and I didn't do anything.'

I started to cry again, and it felt the same way it had every other time, like it wasn't going to get everything out.

'What do you think was happening to her, Ness? I know

you were worried before it happened.'

I thought about what I understood, what I almost knew. 'She was psychotic, I think.'

Minnie's eyes widened slightly and she nodded.

'It sounds so intense,' I said. 'But I think she was. Things weren't making sense, and she wasn't herself.'

I could see Hetty's face whenever I closed my eyes, and it was the face she had made when she showed me that tattoo on her back that wasn't real, the face when she had let Sean go in Yarra Bend Park, the face when we were twelve and she'd told me that a man had come up and touched her out of nowhere at the dam in Kangaroo Ground. Her pretend face, like she was okay. When she clearly hadn't been, hardly ever. I'd been completely wrong about her and that face—it wasn't her okay face. She had been scared, over and over, and hadn't known how to shake me, to make me understand.

'You might be right. But when someone is psychotic, living in an unreality, it's not possible for their best friend to drag them out into the light again.'

My throat filled with grief.

'She didn't give you enough time to understand before she gave up. But it's not your fault and it's not hers.'

'You think she gave up?'

'I don't know, Ness. I think in that moment, when she decided to be in the water, she gave up on anything else that wasn't being in the water.'

I was sure this was true.

'It's okay to be angry about that. She gave up and she left you.'

I hadn't let any anger come through at all, except towards myself. It felt like, if I let myself, I would drop dead or burst into flames or choke. I know now that I was very angry, at Hetty and at her family and at all the men who had let her down; at myself and Dill and Elaine, for not understanding. Nothing comes from anger except more of it, like fire or oil, but it felt good in that moment to let some of it rise.

'Do you remember that day when I was strange at work?' Minnie picked at her nails as she asked this, and furrowed her face a little.

I tried to remember.

'The day I was on the phone here and then I got off and you asked me what was wrong?'

Nothing.

'I think I must have looked worried?'

I remembered then, only a few weeks back, that day when I was worried about Hetty, like I always seemed to be but maybe even more so, and I had seen that Minnie was worried too, about something else, but I'd let her brush me off and ask me about my own things. She always did that, and it seemed she knew she was doing it.

'Yes—yes, I remember! You had this strange phone call. I thought it was Sim being mean or something.'

She laughed. 'Oh, no. No. It wasn't Sim. Thank you for noticing, though.'

'Minnie—you don't have to thank me—I didn't help you! I just let you focus on me.'

'I didn't let you help me.'

She shifted slightly on the stool, to get comfortable or to

give herself some time to prepare. I doubted Minnie had had much practice sharing her own discomfort or sorrow. She was too busy sharing everyone else's, trying to help, feeding and standing by. I watched her shift herself again. She was so pretty.

'I was angry that day. But I'm not very good at anger. My brother called to tell me that he had stopped taking his medication. He imagined I would be excited for him, but of course I wasn't.'

Her hands were folded against her knees.

'He has done it before. And every time, he gets very sick. We make him promise to see his doctor and start again, and to tell us if he needs help, not to just stop the only thing that helps. But he doesn't. Not until it's too late.'

I hadn't known about Minnie's brother other than his name, Eugene. She had told me they were close when they were little, only just over a year apart in age: Minnie the elder one, protective and loving like she was with everyone. I hadn't imagined him sick. He had been bright and well in my mind, safe with such a sister.

'He starts not to make sense. But it's slowly. Like Hetty. No one can help him, because every time he does something unusual, we hope it's the last time.' She looked up at me, her eyes damp. 'I wonder if you were hoping too?'

I nodded, and put my hand on hers. I had been hoping and I wouldn't hope again. Or maybe I would. Minnie was telling me that I would. I placed the idea down deep and swallowed my saliva.

We sat for hours there at the window, and Minnie brought small cold cucumbers with sauce and then lemon snow for us to eat. I wasn't hungry but putting it in my mouth was a distraction. I wanted to tell Hetty how beautiful Minnie was, because I knew she would understand. We had always had similar reactions: our eyes becoming wet at the same moments, our faith in what life meant fuelled by the same things. At least, I had thought so.

GLACIER
frozen river

The next day I booked a ticket home. I told Dill and Minnie: Dill in the Marjorie kitchen, Minnie on the phone. I texted Faith, who replied immediately, asking to see me before I flew.

Toronto felt special in the days after I knew I was leaving, and I went walking to see all the places I'd grown fond of. It had only been nine months, but I felt like I'd lived so long and would never know another city in the same way. I smiled at the people I passed, trying to be airy. Sometimes they smiled back.

Faith and I met to say goodbye on a Saturday morning. The heavens battered my face as I walked towards our favourite cafe on Bloor. Toronto was very different in the winter, for the lack of people, the abandoned patios and the first snow clinging to the gutters like icing sugar. It began quietly to rain ice as I reached College and Bathurst, not cold enough for the real thing, and I tried to enjoy it.

I thought about all the things I wouldn't do before I

left—one last ride on the subway, one last Jamaican patty wrapped in coconut bread, one last visit to Dufferin Mall or Dollarama. I wouldn't go to the gallery and see Emily Carr again; I wouldn't lie on the High Park grass, the greenest I had ever seen. I would go to Tim Horton's at the airport and get a sun-dried-tomato bagel with cream cheese, because that was easy. Dill had insisted I try one, and I was finally getting back my appetite, something small but helpful alongside the grief.

There was no one else in the cafe when I arrived, it being early and rainy and cold. I had my period, and needed to sit down, so I ordered a coffee and a white roll filled with a slice of round meat and some white cheese, and sat where I could see the door. There was no data on my phone and I couldn't see any newspapers or magazines, so I just waited, and when the coffee came I concentrated on just the drinking of it—each sip—so I wouldn't wonder what I would say to Faith when she arrived, and so I could make the most of my second last day in this city. The roll was soft and chewy and the cheese tasted like body, which I liked. I felt the mushed-up bread and animal and off milk travel down my throat when I swallowed, into the rest of me to be processed some more, digested.

I didn't realise Faith was there until she was standing behind the other chair. I hadn't seen her come through the door and to have her close so suddenly pumped my heart.

'Hi,' she said, and pulled out the chair. She began unwrapping a very long scarf from where it was circled around her, and when she had finished, her thin neck bare, she hung it on the back of her seat. The scarf was many colours, but mostly blue. I could see slivers of ice melting along the wool.

After she sat down she smiled, so warmly I almost swooned. I had missed her so much and now I was leaving and she would go on living her life without me and I without her. It felt almost dangerous to be here with her for such a short time, as if it might permanently damage me to remind myself of how good she was. I felt damaged already, though, and pleasure hadn't happened since Hetty had died. I needed some pleasure. Faith's face reminded me of that.

'Would you like a coffee?' I asked, preparing to get up and order her one, to get away from her for a second to gather myself.

She shook her head.

'No?'

'No.'

'What would you like, then?'

She shook her head again, and leaned towards me, just a small amount, so I could smell her chamomile hair. 'I would like to go back to my house with you.'

~

We had sex as soon as Faith had closed the door, up against it, both of us coming quickly and heavily. The blood between my legs didn't matter at all. Like trees filled with water from the sky we shook, and then Faith took off all of my clothes very slowly but didn't touch my skin, and we walked to her bedroom, laid down a towel, and pulled the lilac covers up around us. I asked Faith to be naked with me, and when I let myself look at her beneath the covers I saw how delicate she was, how her stomach was just waiting there, and I started to cry and Faith moved to hold me, the whole of me, until I stopped. When I looked at her after I had finished, there were tears in her eyes and on her cheeks, too, and her mascara had painted two lines down either side of her face. She coughed and then gulped, as if the tears were complicated.

'I'm so sorry,' she said, with a wobbly voice.

I started to shake my head but stopped myself. Hetty was gone. I could let Faith tell me what she felt.

'It's okay,' I replied, pushing back some of her hair that had fallen forward across one eye. 'I'm sorry too.'

~

It was difficult to say goodbye that night, at Faith's low white gate that was falling in on itself. Nothing was actually difficult, compared with losing Hetty, but it was as difficult as it could be without being anything at all.

I stepped my way back to Marjorie and imagined my pupils adjusting as the sky darkened. I felt the loneliness I used to feel at this time of night back in Melbourne, as if everyone in the world was quiet now, and nothing could change that. It felt good to have a feeling that wasn't related to Hetty, and then she was back inside me and I was sad again, turning the corner of Queen and Spadina, looking through the window of McDonald's at people biting at hamburgers and pulling at fries.

Our street was quiet. I was cold despite all my layers and walked quickly, to get to the house and up to the bedroom and the bed, where I would lie down and curl into a ball.

Ahead of me there was something standing. It didn't seem like a person, and the air was thick with dark, so I couldn't see properly. As I neared the thing, I blinked and saw that it was Hetty. From three metres away I could see her, dressed in her Silverchair T-shirt and pyjama pants. She was holding out her arms as if she wanted us to hug, and she wasn't smiling but her face was round and calm.

'Hetty,' I said, loud enough for her to hear.

She didn't move.

'Hetty.'

I stepped towards her, very slowly, trying to make sure my heart slowed down too, from a race to a gallop. She was there, and then I took another step and she was gone, and then I blinked and she was definitely gone, and there was nothing on the ground where she had been, no Silverchair T-shirt or puddle of the outer layers of her. Nothing at all, and I felt my heart start to beat as it normally did, as if I'd never even seen her.

I walked up the steps to Marjorie and unlocked the door, turning once more to see if she was there again on the road so I could go back to her, but she wasn't and I couldn't. That was the last time I ever saw her, and I rubbed my shoulders until the skin hurt on that verandah before I entered: rubbed them for her and for me. It was the beginning of an ending.

Inside, it was warm.

YARRO-YARRO
ever-flowing

When I was eighteen, a few weeks after I'd said goodbye to the flat grey and beige of Ringwood Secondary College—after the Valedictory Dinner and the last cigarette behind Portable C, walking out one last time with relief in my chest and mouth and ears—a group of us met mid-morning at Warrandyte for a swim in the Yarra. There was nothing to do: exams were over, applications for the next part of our lives had been sent, the long summer was in everything like a bad smell. There was nowhere to just be in Ringwood, apart from Eastland or the train station or Lake Park, with its swing set and earnest wooden animal statues.

In Warrandyte you could hide along the water and terrorise the natural habitat for hours. There were so many spots to lay down blankets and stretch out dirty legs, spots behind thick bush where only the brown water would be disturbed. Hetty had told me the night before that Jump Rock had been chosen, because it was a weekday and wouldn't be crowded, and some people wanted to jump it. I packed my duffel bag slowly: sun cream, cashews, vodka in a Cottee's bottle, fading bathers and towel.

One of Hetty's friends, Sam, picked me up in the morning. Hetty was happy when I jumped in, and she climbed through to the backseat briefly to pinch my cheeks and kiss my forehead, telling me we would have fun. Sam wound along Wonga Road with all the windows down, and Hetty's hair whipped in and out of her window with the wind. I loved her as always, and watched her slim freckled arms gesticulate the whole way, as she told Sam her small quiet stories and he listened.

Sam was kind, and handsome, and had never had a girlfriend. Something about his face was so private that I never held his gaze for very long, but I imagined that if I ever kissed a boy it might be him, because of his careful beauty, and because he would hold me slightly back, his palms on my shoulders, neither of us wanting heat or sweat or love from each other, but touching lips because we could.

I wondered what Sam thought about me, and if he ever imagined his skin against mine. I didn't sense the keenness for Hetty coming off him that I did with other boys, their bodies unable to contain their greed. He treated her with dignity and was clearly fond of her, but he didn't watch her, didn't tease her, and she told me she understood the way he was more than the rest of them, because it was uncomplicated.

Sam had been the first to get his licence: he had turned eighteen in January, before our last year of high school had even started, and had driven to school every day of Year Twelve in the second-hand Subaru station wagon his parents had given him. Sometimes he would pick Hetty up, then me, and we would arrive at school in the mornings together. I was calm and important walking through the front gate and past the locker bays with Sam and Hetty. I didn't bother wondering if they felt the same.

I hadn't asked Hetty how many people might be coming to swim with us. When we arrived there were already a few small groups of familiar faces spread across towels and blankets at the edge of the water, just at the spot where the river curved to head towards the Warrandyte Bridge and a wall of rapids. The surrounds of Jump Rock were slightly sinister, though I couldn't quite work out why. We'd come to spend time there often over the years, and maybe it was the constant smell of pot in the air, the empty bottles always scattered around, the danger of the jump that we all felt we should make despite most of us being terrified.

I didn't like how open it was sitting there, and wished we were down at some other more secluded spot. Older couples and young families wandered past with trikes and ice creams and sunscreen, but the seediness prevailed. I felt my breakfast of muesli and Rev mixing in my stomach.

It was hot and bright already but the air wasn't wet, and I hoped that I might be able to avoid getting in the water, putting my shy body on display, asking for eyes. I hadn't had new bathers since I was fourteen, and they were saggy at the bum and faded in dirty spots all over. My pubic hair had tufted out at each side of my groin when I'd tried them on the night before, no matter how I pushed it back in, and I had a pimple on my back that was deep and florid and made me feel oily.

I wanted Hetty to think I was beautiful, to wonder at my body and how I moved it, to want to touch me the way I wanted to touch her. I had hardly admitted to myself how much I wanted to hold her hips and smooth my fingers along the side of her, the length of her, but the want was there and it was only getting stronger. She'd never feel the same about me, I was sure. Reminding her of the whole of me was suddenly uncomfortable.

'Ness, want to sit here?' Hetty asked me, standing on a bit of grass, her face bunched up in the sun.

She'd chosen a spot close to the others, and I let myself look properly, to see who we were with. There were some boys I didn't like much—they were crass and careless in their speech and movements, and had never bothered to know me at all. Jeremy was the loudest and most offensive, yet the most attractive to many of the girls in our year. He'd had brief intimate relationships with about ten of them over the last three years of school, and had dumped each one only after getting with the next one. I knew it was strange I didn't want to be intimate with him, or maybe that wasn't the right word and it was just different. I would have much preferred to lie down in bed next to the girls he had been with—to comfort them, to smooth their hair, to remind them of their power. He didn't have a hold over me, and I didn't want to sit near him, but we spread out a blanket and did, because there was nowhere else, and it wasn't something to protest.

I started drinking early that day and so did Hetty. It had always felt more dangerous to drink near the river, as if I was tempting the water to take me as I slowly inebriated myself. I didn't feel good about finishing school, but I didn't wish it wasn't over either. I wanted to be numb, though when I drank I usually just felt tired and thick before I was able to escape anything.

The warmth of the vodka in my head was helping me drop down into the day, and while Hetty lay down in her bikini and the boys stared at her and kicked at each other and laughed and prepared to dive in, I sat and sipped and looked out at the brown moving water. Sticks and Pacific black ducks and invisible eels floated past. I felt the splash of river on my cheek as the boys hit the water. I was possibly, momentarily, happy.

~

Later, Hetty convinced me to jump off Jump Rock with her. It was on the other side of the river, above the banks of North Warrandyte, and was big enough to edge out onto and stand on: just jutting out from where the bush and the trees clung to the steepness. The rock was at least five or six metres above the water, and though I'd seen so many people jump off it and go under and swim back and laugh as they were drying themselves, I was terrified I would land on the wrong part of the river, where it was shallow and spikes lay just below, or that I wouldn't even jump far enough out to miss the bank and would land on the side of what we had just climbed to get up to it, my face flattened and my body ripped apart.

I'd never been able to rely on my body the way others could on theirs—I didn't know what it was capable of, but had always assumed not much. When Hetty fell over, there never seemed to be a mark left on her skin. I had bruises up and down my legs like lily pads, always, despite never remembering bumping in to anything.

Hetty was languid that day, from the sun and the drink and the eyes of many upon her. She stretched and giggled. She kept her eyes on me, and tried to reason with my long list of fears.

'We'll hold hands,' she said, as if that made a difference.

'But that way I'll just pull you towards the sharp parts with me!'

'There aren't any sharp parts, Ness. It's really deep over there. You'll be fine.'

Sometimes I wondered if she understood me at all.

Her eyes were glassy as we slid into the water. I copied her doggy paddle, because there seemed no better way to get to the other side without starting a freestyle stroke, which would have been far too earnest. She stopped halfway, the top of her hair and her head above the water, and waited for me to catch up, saying again that I would be glad to have done it once I'd jumped and was back in the water again.

We got to the other side, fished ourselves out and clambered up the riverbank. I imagined those who sat back where we had started—those boys with their cruel minds and loose tongues—watching us, comparing our bodies. My unsure parts and my hideous bathers; Hetty's grace. I remember a blush came to my neck imagining what they were saying.

After I slipped trying to get up and into the bush that would bring us around to the rock, Hetty took my hand and gently pulled me. We pushed our way up and through the trees that surrounded the small rock landing, and I felt the heat of the day against my wet skin. It felt pleasant, though I could sense my body had started to understand what I was about to do—my heart was beating quickly and my mouth was dry. My flesh didn't want me to land on something sharp; it wanted me safe down below, lying on a towel. Despite the vodka, I wasn't numb at all. I could feel the wetness of the drooping fabric at my crotch dripping down between my legs.

Hetty was ahead of me, standing and looking over at the water. She turned and smiled at me with big cheeks.

'Come on, Ness—come to the edge. It's beautiful-scary looking out.'

I walked to join her and saw how high we were. My tummy started hitting itself. Hetty leaned against me and I could feel how calm her body was, how still. I tried to take it in where our skin met.

'I'm so glad I'm doing this with you,' she said, as if we were about to change our lives, to venture forth and achieve something. 'I've always wanted to jump off here.'

'I'm really scared,' I told her, and then there was a loud splash and we could see the boys across the river from us, now in the water, playing and fighting.

We looked at each other and I smiled to distract myself. Hetty took a deep breath. I could almost hear it rumble in her lungs. 'I'm scared too, Ness. I'm always scared. Of everything.'

I wanted to ask her what she meant, why she was scared when she was full of all that anyone had ever wanted. I didn't reply, even though I wanted to say: *but how could you be but you shouldn't be but if you're scared then how will I ever not be.*

I needed to jump before I really changed my mind. We

clasped damp hands and took a step back to run forward. I don't remember anything more until I was submerged.

~

Later on it was still warm and Sam lay with us on our blanket. He and Hetty's bodies side by side made me want to avert my eyes, as if they needed privacy. I could smell mull in the wind and sat up to pour some more vodka down my throat, a punishment.

The jump had been horrible, and I wasn't glad when I'd done it and was back in the water. When my body had hit the surface—my chest and breasts first—it had hurt more than I'd anticipated. I tried to remember the drop down but I couldn't. The only part of it that made me glad was the look Hetty gave me when we were both bobbing, wiping the water out of our eyes. She was laughing, and her face was wet and shining. I liked that we had done it together.

I was looking at Sam, his cashew-coloured arms crossed underneath his head to make a pillow, his back warm and his stomach and chest below, when he lifted himself up and looked back at me. I was embarrassed to be caught admiring him, and knew he would know that was what I had been doing. He would be used to being admired, like Hetty.

I smiled to try to make sure my cheeks didn't redden, and he smiled back, then lifted himself up and around to sitting. Hetty lay next to him not moving, a drugged princess. She'd always slept like the dead, or a cried-out baby.

'Should we go get some fish and chips?' Sam asked me. He moved his eyes from mine down to Hetty's still body and back again, raising his eyebrows. 'She'll be out for a while, I reckon.'

I was shy to go for a walk with him. What would either of us say, or do with our hands, I wondered, as I nodded and we pulled ourselves up off our towels to standing. It was easier for me to be around people who were not so self-aware, so watchful and precise as Sam. I wanted him to like me, though I couldn't imagine him disliking anyone. He was too self-contained for that sort of energy. I reminded myself he was shy too, but that he was making an effort. I stood as tall as I could in my body and nodded again.

Hetty didn't stir while we prepared ourselves: scrounging for our wallets in our bags, Sam pulling on a shirt, me a singlet.

'Will she be okay if we're gone when she wakes up?' I asked him, knowing that she would be.

'Yeah.' He smiled lightly, and we turned towards the steep bush hill before the main road.

'Which way?' Sam asked, as we neared the gravel path and the grassy one beside it, both leading up to the street and the chip shop. The grassy one was steeper but more interesting, with a thin track through the weeds made flat and smooth by summer feet. I liked fighting my way up this desire path—the one chosen by the people. I pointed my head at it and shrugged. Sam nodded back.

It was much hotter now we were out from under the shade of the gums that stood near the river, their branches and leaves blocking the sky. The sun beat down and I felt sweat begin to gather between my creases.

Sam began the trail first, carrying his thongs in one hand. His calf muscles pulled and hardened as he moved himself upwards. I kept my thongs on and followed him but the flattened grass of the path was slippery, and I couldn't get beyond a certain point. Sam turned, earlier than someone else might have because he was thoughtful, and when he saw that I was stuck he slid down to help me. He grinned and gestured to my hand, and when I nodded, took it in his. His skin felt like I had imagined it would: sanded and warm.

'Thank you,' I said, and let him move me. I didn't care that I should be climbing this hill myself: it was just nice to be near him. I wondered if he wanted to be touching me, and if I wanted it too. I couldn't feel anything happening in my lower half—not a flicker. But he was even more beautiful up close.

Towards the top we stalled, after Sam placed his foot where there was no solid ground and I wobbled, and we half-fell together against the bleached rim. Laughing, our hands pulling at each other and holding one another up, I watched Sam's face crack open into something more full than I had seen before.

He leaned forward and placed his lips on mine just as I tried to move them. He kissed my mouth and I let his tongue slip my lips apart and in, wet and slightly sticky. My body trembled from knowing he wanted me, trying to work out what I wanted, moving my mouth with his, breathing in the cloy of his saliva and peppery sweat. I felt hot in an unpleasant way, and tried to help him find a rhythm but couldn't.

I pulled my mouth away and wiped it, my eyes on the dirt beneath us and our four feet. Sam moved away from me, and when I looked up I saw his arms were hanging at his sides.

'Shit. I'm sorry,' he said.

'No, don't be.'

'I didn't know if you—' He stopped without interruption, and twisted his hands into a honey-coloured mess. He was someone to feel sorry for, all of a sudden: someone needy and naked. I wanted to be anywhere else.

'It's okay. Don't worry.' I couldn't say anything more than that and so we stood there, and then he moved to pull himself to the top of the hill and I followed, heaving myself politely, until we arrived at the car park opposite the pub. It was unbearably hot now that we were at street level. I imagined being in the water as we crossed the road. I imagined my arms moving back and forth to keep me afloat, alone and able.

Sam suggested he wait and bring the food back, after we had ordered and he had insisted on paying for Chiko Rolls, potato cakes and minimum chips. I breathed out only after I had moved through the plastic curtain straps and was back on the street.

A part of me wished we had kept kissing, that he had lost control and pulled me down into some shrub, that we had fucked in the dirt. I knew, though, that I was only wishing this because I wanted things to go back to how they had been before, and without the conclusion of sex we were just in between, not able to move forward or back. I didn't want him. I knew the more eager he was, the more I would shrink. The thought of him stroking my body glued up my throat.

~

When I got back to the river Hetty was still lying there, her arms and legs and hair spilled out around her. I sat down and looked out across the water, Sam's lips still on mine. I hoped he wasn't too embarrassed or disappointed, though I couldn't imagine he would be. It would have been a chance he took in the moment, and that was all. I was sure I wasn't something to get over. I wondered if I would tell Hetty, and what she might say if I did. Beside me, she moved, then made a sighing noise and opened her eyes. She lifted herself up and yawned, stretching out her legs and leaning forward to meet them.

My vodka was next to me, forgotten, and I lifted it and drank. It was very warm now, and parts of my body became slightly less shaky immediately—my arms, my stomach, my toes. I sat still, waiting for Hetty to say something because I couldn't. The air around us was barely moving, and my thighs were shiny.

'Should we try to find some water ribbons?' Hetty asked brightly, then yawned again.

Hetty was obsessed with water ribbons. Ever since we had learned about bush foods in Year Nine History with Ms Diaz, how they grew all over Victoria and how you could eat them if you knew how to choose the right parts, she'd been looking, trying to find something we had read about to see what it tasted like, and imagine what it would have been like in Australia before the British arrived.

I had gently reminded her so many times that we would never be able to know what it was like, to understand the country we were born in, because it had been changed too much and we hadn't listened properly when we got here, rushing to settle and make and change when there had been no need. Hetty told me she knew, that she wasn't really pretending it was easy, but she still wanted to eat something that had grown indigenously from the Australian ground.

We searched in Tecoma for pink native raspberries, and drove all the way to the Strzelecki Ranges to look for the tubers of the wombat berry, which we did find, and cooked up that night into a stringy, mild casserole. Every time we had come to swim in or walk beside the Yarra in Warrandyte, Hetty had looked for water ribbons along the banks—they liked to grow in the muddy bits where the water had stilled. She had a colour photo showing what they looked like growing against water, and it lived in the front pocket of her backpack, bent and smudged. They were beautiful, half-standing and half-floating, long against the top of the water. You could eat the little green fruits that gathered under the tiny flowers in a spike at the top of them, and the tubers that sat at their bottoms.

'Yeah, go on then,' I said 'But we better wait for Sam. He's bringing back fish and chips.'

'Ooh,' Hetty said, though I doubted she would indulge in much of it.

I waited to see whether my mouth would open again, to tell her about Sam. I was sure she would be kind, and wouldn't make things difficult when he got back, with stares and smiles and giggles, but I didn't feel I could talk about why I hadn't wanted it.

Hetty was standing now, and had pulled her dress on over her bathers. 'If we go now, we might be back before him,' she said.

'We very well might be.'

As we climbed up to the path and stood dusting the grass and the dirt off our backs and bottoms, Hetty took the photograph out of her bag.

'Where did you get that again?' I asked, pointing at it.

'My dad took it,' she answered, trying to smooth out the photo with one hand. 'When he was living in Gippsland.'

I didn't ask more. Hetty's dad was tricky—for her, for her family, for me as someone on the near outside, looking in. He was angry and sad and loving and slow and often full of alcohol, which made him unpredictable. That he clearly loved Hetty more than he loved anyone else was unhealthy, and seemed to be her blind spot. She talked about his time living on his own in Gippsland when she and her siblings were small as if it had been a romantic pilgrimage, rather than what I believed—that he had run away, unable to handle reality. I respected her need to leave him unexamined, but I couldn't join her.

'He gave it to me because he thought I'd like to see them floating on the water and know what they were called. The leaves aren't as wide in Gippsland. But otherwise we should look for something like that.'

I suggested we start moving, as the sun would soon start to slowly sink down and become pink and then nothing below the trees. As we edged along, I watched Hetty in front of me, the tendons in her back bulging and pulling as she pushed past trees and weeds. I could smell the thick sweat of the mud and the sweetness of the plants we were passing, and I let my eyes move towards the bank to watch for something like the shrub in the photograph.

It was starting to rain, very lightly, when I heard Hetty yell out and then saw her trundle down the bank, right to the edge of the water.

'There!' she said, and got on her knees to lean forward.

I joined her at the edge of the river and saw what she was

trying to touch—a plant with light-green stand-up leaves, some with conifer-shaped endings, and below the standing leaves a fan of long, slim ribbon leaves floating in the water.

'They really are water ribbons,' I said, and Hetty looked up at me with such a smile that the whole of me lifted slightly.

'As if someone just dropped some green ribbons into the water,' she said, and leaned down to touch one of the floating leaves. 'They feel strong.'

Hetty took the photo out of her pocket and smoothed it out again to see if we were right.

'Yes! It looks the same. Just with thicker leaves, like Dad said.'

She handed me the photo and leaned forward again, towards the strong plant, in the home it had made against the soil wall and the water. It did look like we had found one—the picture had thinner leaves but it was standing in the same tall drooping way, and the tufts at the top, like tiny white and yellow trees, were similar. I looked closer and could see the few leaves that were swimming along the top of the brown Yarra water. It smelt like garden, and I watched Hetty take photos on her small, broken phone, likely to show her father.

'I don't want to destroy it,' she said, after she had stood and was back with me again, somewhat past the wonder.

'We don't have to.'

She looked at me and scrunched her face. 'But I want to try to eat the tuber potatoes at the ends! And the little fruits. Maybe if we just pull out a part of it? Or will that kill the whole thing? I don't want to ruin something that was living happily on its own.'

I shrugged. 'It doesn't matter, Het. It'll be our dinner. I'm sure there are other water ribbons along here that can move in if we take this one.'

She was still looking at where the plant stood, where it floated.

'I know that's not actually a thing. That another water ribbon plant will just see this vacant lot and move in. But really, let's just do it; it's fine, really—' I said, waiting for her to turn back around.

'Yes!' she said, turning with a smile, then moving towards me. 'You always make things clear again.'

With Hetty's arm around my shoulder, I felt good, and imagined the tubers and the fruits would be delicious, in a subtle, unusual way, and that we would enjoy eating them together because it was a moment we had been waiting for. We took our shoes off and I rolled up my pants. Hetty gathered her skirt up around her waist and tied it in front like a belt, and we stepped into the water.

'Maybe if I pull it from the bottom? From the roots?' Hetty asked, and I nodded.

She moved her whole arm down into the water and stuck her tongue out the side of her mouth with concentration, trying to find the obvious end—the place that helped the plant to grow. It took a few dunks of her arm, and a few grabbings around at the bottom of the river, before she smiled and jerked her whole body to pull it free.

'Got it!' she yelled to me. 'It's really muddy down there. Muddling.'

I did a small silly dance, and then took the long, dripping

plant with its hairy, intricate end and handed Hetty a towel to dry herself.

'It didn't want to come with me,' she said. 'Maybe I should have listened and let it be.'

'No, Hetty. Don't worry.'

I swung the water ribbon over my shoulder, the tubers and root veins hanging behind me near the small of my back, and we walked along to where we had started, where Sam was lying down with his eyes closed: perhaps sleeping, perhaps pretending to be. The sun was beginning to set, it was almost summer dusk, and I saw the wrapped grey paper next to him, full of fried food. My stomach muttered.

~

Later that night, after Sam had dropped us off and I had managed to catch his face to smile in a way I hoped was tender, Hetty and I sat on the floor of her bedroom and stroked the water-ribbon leaves.

'I don't want to eat it,' Hetty said.

'That's because you're not hungry,' I answered.

'Know-it-all,' she said, and stretched back along the carpet with a sigh. I could hear her breathing. 'I wish I could show Dad,' she said, lifting her legs up into the air and her arms to meet them.

'Why can't you?'

'Because he's sick. He's not here. He's staying with his brother until he's better.'

'What kind of sick?' I asked, quietly, so she wouldn't feel she had to answer me.

She dropped her legs and arms down, and looked at me from where she lay.

'I don't really know. He was getting angry before he left. And I think he's started drinking in the mornings again.'

I supposed Hetty was scared all the time because she wasn't safe, and that Hetty's mother and sisters and brothers were all scared all of the time too, and I felt callous for thinking she might not have been, that she was luckier and happier than I was. Her lofty voice and her lightness—that wasn't all of her. I tried to think of something helpful to say for a long time, and she beat me to it.

'You don't need to say anything, Nessy. I'm stronger than you think.' She smiled, and with her thin wrist against the knotted rug patted the space beside her. I lay down and we stretched, then sung 'Hey Jude': Hetty beginning with a low sweet drone, and both of us ending the chorus as one.

I stayed the night in Hetty's king single bed, listening to her breath become as fluid as silk after we turned the light off. In the morning we cooked the tubers in the oven and ate the small crisp fruits while we waited. They tasted like sugar water and something unripe. The tubers were soft and narrow, and could have been swedes.

A BILLABONG IS A DEAD RIVER

Hetty has moved through me like water since Toronto. It's three years since I last saw her, really saw her, at the Eaton Centre food court, eating that salad with a gnashing mouth and her eyes wild. I know I'll never stop wishing we had met again, but I tell her what I want to tell her in my dreams.

Leaving Toronto a few weeks after Hetty died was deceptively easy. I suppose when you board you never know how it will feel at the end of a flight, or in the days before you take a taxi to the airport. I could hear something deep inside me trying to tell me to slow down as I packed up our room at Marjorie and chose which of Hetty's dresses I would take with me, because I couldn't leave them all. Despite this, I rushed it. Maybe I couldn't process another ending after such a brutal one had been forced upon me. Maybe I knew I wouldn't be able to say goodbye the best way or the right way, that I didn't have the energy. The only thing I did consciously in those few weeks was let myself float; and I said goodbye to Dill and Minnie near the check-in desk with numb arms and cold cheeks.

I didn't sleep at all on the plane, and spent my seven-hour stopover at LAX lying on the floor in a corner of the transit lounge with one of Hetty's dresses over me and another rolled up under my head for a pillow. I was so sad, but I couldn't cry anymore. Fabric that had touched Hetty's skin was comforting, and I hoped I would be unapproachable beneath my soft paisley shield.

During the second flight I watched the plane move slowly across the world on the tiny TV screen, and when I could see that we were finally flying above Australia I pulled up the arch of the window shade next to me to quickly see something brown and arid, or the floor of red dust I had told myself I had missed so much, but all I could see were cloud beds.

I imagined the flight attendants were being particularly kind to me because I was so clearly vulnerable, damaged, though they were just doing their job and doing it well. They brought me an extra blanket and a chocolate muffin in silver wrapping as we started to circle the edges of Melbourne, the sun rising and the yellow light warming my face as if it knew me. I could see that brown ground and those parched trees, the ones I wanted. I could feel something in me move: just the smallest amount.

There was no grand hurrah when I breathed in the Melbourne air after walking out the airport doors. It was as if nothing had happened.

~

I kept going, which was unexpected, and yet of course I did. Grief is thick, and I didn't know this until I was in it, struggling to get to the edge or at least find a way to thin it out, with water or vinegar or air. It was the first proper grief I'd known, and I felt how it stopped all the normal things for longer and shorter than you would expect—I lost ten kilograms because I wasn't hungry, and then one day, three months after I got back to Melbourne, I ordered fried eggs and bacon and beans and bread at a cafe and ate all of it, with two coffees and a slice of apple cake. I cried many times a day, was soaked in tears, and then a week had gone past and I hadn't cried at all, though the pain was still as fresh as a knife wound when it came. I didn't talk about it—when my mum asked me what had actually happened, wanting to understand the tragedy and be with me beside it, I snapped at her, so she didn't ask me again and then I was telling her everything, it was pouring out of me, and she let me cry all over her chest like I did when I was a toddler and she had fed me milk and put me to bed. I was unpredictable and loose in those first few months, expecting little of myself and nothing of others. Those around me weren't Hetty and never could be. Hetty was all I wanted.

~

Hetty's family held a memorial at a funeral home in Mitcham a few days after I landed. It was a large cold building that smelt like disinfectant, and I arrived early on the morning of the service in Hetty's only black dress to see the place filled with people I knew and who had known her. Every person who walked in—faces held still and eyes blank, like dead fish— reminded me how connected Hetty and I had been. We had lived the same life differently and had shared everything that could possibly be shared.

Hetty's father spoke and he was drunk, and the words slurred and echoed around the great white room. I supposed he was refusing to truly feel the loss of her by numbing himself. He laughed near the end, then held his face with his puffy purple hands and left the podium guided by Hetty's mum. I couldn't hate him, even though I knew he'd been the type of parent who can damage a child, and I suspected that he would never stop injuring those around him.

I had been asked to speak, and I did briefly and with a thick throat. It was difficult and unnerving, as if I was acting out a monologue and making the whole thing about me.

Afterwards there were oval plum cakes and white-bread mayonnaise sandwiches with no crusts. I imagined someone that morning, solemnly cutting each brown edge off, a pile getting higher in the bin beside them. I stood near one of the tables covered with a white tablecloth and held a teacup full of coffee to pretend I was doing something, watching all the people I knew because of Hetty move slowly around, talking quietly to one another without saying anything.

Hetty's parents came to me and looked at me with their pale, hurt eyes, and I felt as if I had killed her. Hetty's mother, Patricia, was beautiful in her high-necked blouse and trousers. She had her elegant hand on her husband's shoulder, almost certainly to steady him.

'Vanessa.'

She had always called me Ness before.

'Patricia. I'm so sorry,' I said, choked. Nothing could come out that day without a wave of salty tears following just behind. I didn't even feel sad—just awash with water.

She flinched slightly at my sorry, and I knew it wasn't enough or right or helpful, but I didn't have anything else I could give her. Patricia hadn't been around much when we were growing up—she worked because Hetty's father couldn't. There were too many children and too much hope had gone into creating a family they couldn't actually hold together properly. So she had worked hard as a school principal in Glen Waverley, and had come home late with piles of things to read and decisions to make that had nothing to do with any of them; would kiss each child absentmindedly on the head and ask after them wearily, fixing a simple dinner with her sensible, clipped-nail fingers.

I'd never been told how Patricia and Hetty's father, Vince, had found each other in their beginning, but I appreciated how after they had found each other they had held on to one another for so long. They were so different, in every conceivable way, and it bolstered them somehow. I had decided years ago that their differences were Hetty—what made her so interesting, so near to magical. She was a contradiction, a tricky sum: the best and the worst of everything.

I watched Patricia's face as it moved into a half-smile. She didn't hate me, perhaps, or maybe she was just too tired and sad to be able to know what she felt. It didn't matter anyway. Hetty was gone. All there was left was anger and sadness and fatigue. We would never see the other side.

'Thank you.' She moved a tissue up to her eyes and dabbed at one. They were glistening as if there would always be tears in them, waiting to fall. She stepped towards me, leaving Vince to stand on his own.

'And you mustn't blame yourself, dear girl. You know that.'

My heart bulged and pushed against my ribs. I looked at Patricia's face all over, and then at Vince's behind her, and all I could see on each of them was grief and resignation. Maybe they knew how much I'd loved Hetty, and how she could slip out of your hands before you had learned how to catch her.

Vince's body shuddered a little, like a car starting up after a long time idle, and he moved towards me and took my hands in his warm, swollen ones. I could smell alcohol—bourbon or rum, something like honey—and I saw how red the whites of his eyes were, as if they were bleeding, which I supposed that they were, in a way.

'She loved you,' he said, his sweet breath thick around our faces. 'And you loved her.' Then he let himself sway, or the swaying overcame him, and he stepped back towards Patricia, who took his arm again.

I wanted to say thank you, thank you. Thank you for creating such a wonderful creature. Thank you for understanding how much I cared. Instead I nodded, letting the tears collect in my head like rain in a spout full of leaves, and hoped my eyes could tell them.

As they moved away, after patting my arm and telling me to keep in touch, I could see the loss in each of their backs and in their limbs and their tread, weighing down their shoulders and blocking out most of the sounds around them. I could see how Hetty had lived inside them, and how she always would, but that she was dead everywhere else, and how that made it terrible.

That night I couldn't sleep, so I listened to the ABC on the radio in my old bedroom—now my parents' spare room, for the visitors they never had. My heart ached when I thought of my mother hoping someone would need to come and stay there, with them, and realising as the years went on that no one ever would. My heart ached for my parents, who had probably wanted more than just one miserable child, and certainly hadn't planned a life filled with sickness and silence. When I pushed away that ache, there was the ache of Hetty behind it, and I tried not to wonder, again, how sad she might have felt as she walked into that lake, as she dived into something so cold and lonely and untamed.

I made myself a snack in the kitchen at four in the morning—biscuits with sliced cheese and white-fleshed tomatoes and powdered pepper. I pushed the aches away again with crisp and wet.

~

It took six months for me to remember that I'd built a sort of existence for myself in Toronto that wasn't Hetty, and to wonder if maybe I could do that again. It was as if one morning I shook my head and something came loose: something valuable. I bought a phone and joined Facebook and asked for the people I had added as friends to send me their numbers. I went to a party, wearing something nice for the first time since Hetty's funeral, trying to inhabit the clothes instead of letting them just hang against me, and stood near a wall with a plastic cup of riesling.

It was the birthday of a friend from a job I had before we left for Toronto, at a delicatessen where old men sat and ate baguettes and drank dark coffee for hours, and no one under the age of forty cared to enter. We had worked there together only for a few months, but had liked each other and been able to tell each other that in a way, and I was glad she still wanted to know me. Her name was Molly, and she had long blond curled hair and big teeth and smelt like oranges.

That party was insignificant except for the way I moved differently in my velvet dress; but then I was invited to another party where we sat down for a meal together halfway through, and Molly was there with her friend Voula, who was tall and wide and calm, with dark lips and short hair licking the nape of her broad neck. Voula asked me home with her after that dinner, that party where we were butternut-squash soup and sliced pumpernickel, followed by burnt steak with creamed potatoes. We kissed in the taxi on the way, and she led me up the stairs to her flat with one large warm hand. It was months before I told her about Hetty, because I didn't need to. When I did she pulled me in and kissed my temples.

I thought about Faith and Hetty at the beginning when I made love to Voula, but only when my eyes were closed and my nose wasn't near her skin. She was so different to those two—her eyes never looking away, her smell as confident as liquorice. She didn't hide or apologise for herself, ever. It was scary and exciting, and ultimately what I needed. She held me and held herself as if we were powerful, never broken, worth the time.

Voula had a family that loved her with words and touch and

song and gifts and acts of service: all of the ways. I had decided when I came back to Australia that I would see my parents more, but when I met Voula's large, passionate mother and her kind, crinkled father, I compared them with mine and felt a familiar disappointment.

I moved into her small flat and read every small scrap of paper she had tacked to its surfaces. Voula had studied philosophy at university and wanted to hold on to the ideas that had excited her. My favourite was in her handwriting, rounded and sure, on a piece of cream paper ripped along one side and faded, stuck to the top of her bedroom mirror. It read: ALL IS FLUX.

I told her I liked it and she smiled.

'It's Heraclitus. He might be my favourite. He said that change is unavoidable. You know that famous quote "This river I step in"?'

I was back in Toronto, walking with Faith across that bridge with those words arched above it, that viaduct that did not help us over water but rather was our path towards it.

I hadn't wanted Hetty to change, I realised. I hadn't wanted our relationship to change. Even though I had chosen to go to the other side of the world with her, I hadn't wanted the backdrop of our story ever to change. When I knew I loved her and didn't let it out, when I realised we might not want the same things anymore but didn't talk to her about it, I was trying to stop the flow. But the flow, the current, was unavoidable.

I told Voula this and she looked at me reassuringly. 'Oh, yes. We all go through it, Ness. It must take a lifetime to accept that we can't stop the waves from coming.'

~

Time moved on, as it does; as I had forgotten when Hetty died, despite my body propelling me forward. I started to understand that I had been through a lot, that I could only be kind to myself. I can now think of Hetty without crying, though there are still moments when I wail.

I make sure that those around me know who she was, and I don't accept any shame in myself for the love I had for her. Voula helps me do this: encourages me to stand by the feelings I had for Hetty. It feels like letting go and holding on.

Acknowledgments

First of all, I have to say a very heartfelt thank you to the Text Publishing team. I still can't really believe that a company I dreamed of working with has published my book, and I feel incredibly lucky to have had such dedicated publishing support. To my editor, David Winter—you have shown me so much more than just how to edit, how to work collaboratively on a manuscript, and how to make a fledgling novel draft a grown, real thing. My time spent working on *Cherry* with you has finally convinced me that a marathon can be much more satisfying than a sprint. Thank you. To Imogen Stubbs, who designed my special cover—thank you for your tireless efforts in getting this right. You are so talented. To my publicist, Jamila Khodja, and to Nadja Poljo, a former Text publicist, who is the reason I got this chance in the first place—endless thanks.

To the publishers and editors and readers of the Australian journals that backed my short fiction over the last five years: you do the most important creative work, and I cannot thank you enough for your commitment and devotion to the written word. A special thanks to Daniel Young of the late *Tincture Journal* and Michele Seminara of *Verity La*, for being two of the kindest and most passionate people I've ever known.

Thank you to my dear old friends for being my sticks and rocks, and for entertaining the frivolous pursuit of fiction: Calida, Carly, Annie, Katie, Kav, Isabel, Joel, Karl, Adnan, Alice, Nic and Rachel, and Luke. To the precious pals I have made in writing and online communities across the world, thank you for making life much more interesting, especially Dom and Zoë, who read early chapters of *Cherry*; André, who has helped with short stories along the way; and Marta, Claire, Anna, Robbie, Lachlan, and Dafna, for cheering me along and letting me do the same for them. Enormous thanks also to the first readers of *Cherry*, who were generous enough to take on the task: Ellena Savage, Jennifer Down, Laura Elizabeth Woollett, and Emily Bitto.

To the beautiful counselling team of wise, strong women at PANDA—I am so lucky to have you in my life and to work alongside you every week. My spiritual wellbeing has never been so high!

Since I was little my mother and father, Carmel and Peter, have shown me that a life lived with your nose in a book can be the most exciting kind of life, and I thank them for this, and for being such softhearted, supportive, spirited, and curious parents and role models. To my brother, Alexander—thanks for putting up with me: I love you! To Petra, Hans, Karl, and Hannah—thank you for welcoming me into your family with such open arms. To my granny and grandpa, Helen and Max, and my nan, Helen, and dearly departed pa, Bob, thank you for everything. And to the grandmother I never met, my mother's mother, Marjorie—thank you for shining a clear light across and beyond your life. You mean so much to me.

This book is also dedicated to Otto Henkell, who was by my side, holding my hand and tending to my heart, over the time I spent writing it. Never have I known a more generous, compassionate or thoughtful person, and never has anyone helped me to feel so grounded and free. Thank you for being there. Without you, this book would not exist.